OPERATION DISASTER!

By
MILTON LESSER

(Originally writing as
Darius John Granger)

ARMCHAIR FICTION
PO Box 4369, Medford, Oregon 97504

For more information about Armchair Books and products, visit our website at...

www.armchairfiction.com

Or email us at...

armchairfiction@yahoo.com

SUPERNOVA!

The Purnamese were known to be sun-worshippers, but their sun was on the verge of destroying them. Their world was doomed—a massive supernova was inevitable. Already having moved several times to planets further out from their increasingly unstable sun, the Purnamese culture started breaking down. Some fought against the forced migrations, fought hard with old beliefs, older customs—and they weren't afraid to spill blood!

Faced with catastrophe and fast losing hold of whatever civilization they had left, two hundred million Purnamese fought to survive while a task force from Earth toiled to save their doomed culture and bring them into an intergalactic brotherhood with the rest of mankind.

FOR A SECOND COMPLETE NOVEL, TURN TO PAGE 83

CAST OF CHARACTERS

MARC CHANNING
He was hated and scorned because of his father's name. Now this doomed world needed him to follow in his father's footsteps.

OTTO SPADE
He was on the first mission a decade ago, and that mission had failed—horribly. Would history repeat itself?

HERBERT FULLER
He was a civilized man with a civilized job from a civilized world. And the only guy standing in the way of the mutineer's freedom.

MANDIT KARR
This peg-legged alien military hero found himself back in uniform and ordered to destroy the only god he believed in!

SUSAN JAMISON
Kidnapped and threatened with torture, she could only hope that somebody would find her soon!

CAPTAIN MACCREADY
He was a big, strong bully of a captain. But how do you stop a crew of murderers with nothing to lose?

BAH-CH'NANQ
This mad High Priest was losing control over his people…and he was willing to literally dismember someone to stop it.

CHAPTER ONE

MARK CHANNING first saw the Operation Disaster starship from the interurban helicopter, which ferried him from Omaha to the starfield. Down below as they hovered, the starship was a big beetle shape, reflecting the silver-blue of the sky. Mark Channing gazed in awestruck wonder: he had seen the interplanetary spaceships many times before, the slender, projectile-shaped vessels, which plied the orbital spacelanes of the solar system. But he had never seen a really big ship like the Operation Disaster starship before.

Operation Disaster!

It had to be big. It was Operation Disaster, wasn't it? It was a ship too ponderous, too massive for the frequent atmosphere thrusts of interplanetary traveling; it was an interstellar ship. And it would take Mark Channing across two thousand light years of space—really deep space—to a planet he had never seen, circling a star that was invisible from Earth except through telescopes. Suddenly, Mark sobered, thinking that soon that star *would* become visible—catastrophically—although thanks to the finite speed of light Earth wouldn't see the effects for two thousand years.

Then Mark was swept up in the excitement of landing, of walking swiftly across the glazed expanse of the starfield while the eyes of the helicopter's more mundane passengers, those bound for merely interplanetary destinations, were riveted on him, of approaching the Operation Disaster starship, from the ground and truly seeing for the first time its enormous size, of making his way through the scurrying jumper-clad ground crew and to the entry-ramp, of climbing the ramp and all at once squaring his shoulders because he was Anson Channing's son and Anson Channing had perished, when Mark was an infant, on a previous Operation Disaster flight to the very same planet; of being swallowed by the huge maw of the starship and gazing in wonderment at the almost cavernous interior of the vessel that would take him across the gulf of deep space in the footsteps of his dead father...

"You're Mark Channing, aren't you?" a rasping voice called from nearby.

Mark blinked against the unexpectedly fierce light coming from the storage hatches to the left of the catwalk that would take him arearship to the specialist quarters, and saw a short, gnarled man with an incredible breadth of shoulders and a face carved, it seemed, from the craggy bedrock of a planet, and a shock of vivid orange hair beginning to gray in streaks. The man had a chest to match his shoulders and was bare-chested and sweaty and leathery-looking. Mark took him for a work-gang boss and said, "Yes, I'm Channing. But I'm sorry, I don't think we've met."

"Otto Spade," rasped the man with the craggy face, the giant's torso and the unexpectedly spindly legs. "Your dad and me were great friends. I'd have known that face anywhere, Mark. You look like your old man."

"You knew Anson Channing?" Mark asked, astonished. The mere acquaintance did not astonish him: it was Otto Spade's attitude, for Spade was friendly, wasn't he? Had Mark ever met anyone directly connected with Operation Disaster work before who had been friendly when informed that Mark was the dead Anson Channing's son? Mark shook his head: the answer was no.

"Knew him?" said Otto Spade, coming nimbly to the catwalk and gripping Mark's hand powerfully. His voice was both friendly and defiant. "Hell, yes, I knew Anson Channing, and a better man never left Earth for deep space!"

MARK FELT his eyes fill, and hated himself for his inability to control his emotions.

"You really mean that?" Mark asked tremulously.

"You've got a million things to do, boy," Otto Spade replied. "You don't want to chew the rag with a crewman now. You're from the Academy, a specialist—"

"There isn't anybody I'd rather talk to—"

"Well, a word of advice, son. I haven't kept secret my feelings about Anson Channing and I don't think you ought to give folks a chance to start thinking Anson Channing's son has no use for anybody but the old man's cronies. You understand?"

"Yes, but—"

"Besides, I'm crew and you're specialist and crew and specialists don't mix."

"But—but weren't you crew when you knew my dad?"

"I came out of the Academy, just like you," Otto Spade said, his voice still rasping impersonally but a wistful look sweeping momentarily across his eyes. "Forty years ago, it was. I served fifteen years in deep space as an Operation Disaster agent with your father, boy. Then they tore up my license."

"But why?" Mark gasped.

Otto Spade answered the question with another, "Why did your father die?"

"I don't know!" Mark cried. "I know what they say, but…"

Spade asked abruptly: "Is that why you're going to Purname?"

"You ought to know better than that!" Mark flushed hotly. "The Academy teaches you to be impersonal and objective, disavowing personal considerations in the face of the goals of your Operation Disaster mission…"

Spade smiled. "See what I mean? I was just making a point of it, boy. Personal considerations aren't supposed to count, but your first moments aboard your first Operation Disaster ship are spent with someone who knew your father. How does that look to you?"

Mark turned away swiftly, stalking up the catwalk. Any answer he gave would be an admission of weakness. But before he'd gone three strides, Otto Spade's big hand fell on his shoulder. "Only making a point, boy. You ought to know if you need a friend on your first assignment, I'm the man. But you ought to use your head about what I told you, too."

"Yes," Mark said. "Thank you."

"And one more thing. Jamison's child is on this ship, Mark."

"Hurley Jamison? I—I didn't know he had any."

"One child, trained in the Academy like you."

"Funny, I never met—"

"You know how Hurley Jamison's family feels about your old man."

"I've heard."

"Anson Channing was responsible for the Purnamese disaster, twenty years ago. That's what they say."

Mark clutched the misshapen man's arm in a savage grip. "Was he?"

"I don't think so," Otto Spade said evenly. "But maybe you'll find out—on Purname." Then, abruptly, he turned back to the loading crew, convicts, mostly, from the nearby penal institution.

"All right, you lazy, gold-bricking, earth-lubbing sons! Get your duffs back under those hauling nets, what you think we have, a whole sidereal year to do the job? Get a move..."

THE RASPING voice faded and disappeared in the general noise of loading, the creaking of booms and winches, the metallic ring of magnet-shod feet as the ground crew swarmed all over the starship's hull, checking every last wire of the intricate cybernetics control unit. The hum of a hundred voices merged to give a hundred sets of orders, the shuffling of sneaker-clad convict feet loading the ship; convicts who would make up its crew because free men did not want to give up a year of their life each way on the long interstellar voyage, unless they were dedicated men like the Operation Disaster agents.

Mark followed the catwalk to the rear of the ship, and here everything was different. Mark saw several lounging figures, passing the final few minutes before blastoff and the long sleep in small talk or a final drink or two, Mark recognized none of the faces: naturally, there wouldn't be more than a handful of first year men like himself aboard the starship. There was no bustle of last-minute preparations in the agent-quarters of the starship: after a final hour or so of waiting the agents would bed down in their long-sleep hammocks, breathe the gas that would slow their metabolic rates almost to the point of death, and spend the year-long journey across deep space to Purname in suspended animation. Meanwhile, of course, the sleep-thinking machinery would be feeding them every tidbit of information they had to know about Purname and the Purnamese situation. They would all be experts by the time they arrived, and it would be as if only a restful night of sleep had elapsed.

Mark presented his credentials to one of the long-sleep technicians, an asthmatic-looking young fellow who seemed completely indifferent to Mark's name as he scrawled something on Mark's Form 15 card and said, "That will be section G, George, sir."

"Can I go to sleep any time?"

"Sure. Just strap yourself in and press the red button," the technician said, looking puzzled. "Most of the agents like to see the blastoff, though. You're allowed. Then they like to talk and drink and have a little party before they sleep a year of their lives away. And usually, they have to be coaxed to bed. But you—"

"Thanks for the information," Mark said gruffly, and was immediately sorry. The young fellow had merely been expressing his amazement, and that was natural enough. Mark wasn't going to tell him that he had nothing in common with the other agents, who probably thought of him—if they thought of him at all—as the son of a pariah.

Mark left the technician and walked across a salon toward a companionway door marked *E-H Sleeping quarters.* Half a dozen agents lounged in the salon, talking and drinking. Occasional soft laughter came to Mark's ears. Music was playing softly and a couple of the agents, a tall man and a short, stocky woman, were dancing. One of those lounging around with drinks in their hands, Mark noticed, was also a girl.

The music became muted, the lights dimmed, and a voice sang:

Polaris to Antares,
My love, my love, he's

A rovin' man!

It was a refrain from the Milky Way Blues, and Mark saw the dancing couple kiss quickly and glide off into the shadows in one corner of the salon. The music swelled in volume as Mark approached the companionway door, his loneliness clinging to him like a sodden cloak. And a voice called:

"Channing!"

HE WHIRLED. The voice seemed to draw him back to the world. Someone was striding toward him through the dimness. It was the second girl, the one who had been lounging in a small group of agents, talking and sipping a drink. She was young, Mark saw, and looked pretty in the dim light. He thought her hair was auburn: no, he amended that, copper colored. Her race was in shadow, but had lovely contours. He was quite sure he had never seen her before.

"In a hurry to sleep?" she asked him. Her voice was soft, almost melodious, yet Mark got the impression she was baiting him.

"Have to get it over with sooner or later," he said. "I don't know you, do I?"

The girl said, still softly, "I know you. I'd know that face anywhere. You look so like the pictures I've seen of your father."

Mark smiled. "You're the second person who's told me that aboard ship."

The girl's voice changed almost to a whisper as she came very close to him and said, "I hope the first one was a man. I hope he punched you in the face. I hope he hurt you."

"What—" Mark gasped.

The girl went on. "Hasn't one Channing done enough damage in the Operation Disaster Corps? Hasn't one Channing caused enough trouble on Purname already?"

Mark replied harshly, "You don't know what you're talking about."

"What you really mean is you'd rather not face it. Did you think anybody wanted you at the Academy, Channing?"

"I did my work."

"Your work! Your father wasn't exactly a credit to the Corps, was he?"

"Why do you hate him so?" Mark asked suddenly. "You're no older than I am. You couldn't have known him. You couldn't possibly know the real story of what happened on Purname twenty years ago, since no one does. You—"

"Everyone knows the real story, Channing. Except you."

"The real story!" Mark cried hotly. "The story old Hurley Jamison left in his notes, you mean. But everyone knew old man Jamison hated my father for some reason, everyone knew Jamison's story couldn't be relied on, everyone knew..."

"Hurley Jamison didn't hate your father any more or less than any other loyal Corpsman. And he wasn't an old man when he died. Don't speak of him like that. He was a young man with dreams and visions and hopes. He— never mind about him. But he knew, as everyone else knows now, that your father violated the code of Operation Disaster by—"

"By trying to save a people too mixed up to save itself!" yelled Mark.

"Stop shouting. They're looking at you. I was saying," she went on coldly, "everyone knows your father violated the code of Operation Disaster by meddling in the Purnamese religious beliefs and finally making them rise up and kill the entire expedition."

"That's hearsay! And besides, the Purnamese *were* evacuated to their outermost planet twenty years ago, as they had to be. Don't you see," Mark said, almost pleading, "that the Purnamese situation is a cosmic irony. The Purnamese are sun-worshippers—and their sun is destroying them."

"I only know what I learned in the Academy. Have you forgotten that, already?"

"No, but sometimes a man has to act according to the dictates of his own reason, even if he violates—"

"Like your father?"

"Like my father, yes."

"No matter who it hurts, who it kills?"

Mark did not answer. He wished suddenly that the year of sleep, not yet begun, was over—wished that they had reached Purname where, maybe, he would find some real answers.

"I said, no matter who it hurts and kills?"

Still Mark did not answer. "I'm Susan Jamison," the girl said.

MARK OPENED the companionway door and rushed through before it had irised fully open. He heard the shutter-like sound of the door closing behind him, and began to run. The music, the Milky Way Blues, rang in his ears. It was being piped all over the ship.

Drink to the rover
on the radar track,

He'll never come back...

Anson Channing had never come back. Hurley Jamison had never come back. A whole expedition, there on far Purname, had perished. Except for Otto Spade, who wasn't talking, Otto Spade, who had drifted free of the wreck of a world, like Melville's Ishmael...

With Hurley Jamison's logbook. What hatred had been kindled between the two men, his father and the girl's father, both dead now, on far Purname? wondered Mark. Hatred to make Jamison lie—

If Jamison had been lying...Because let's face it, Mark, you don't know, you can't be sure.

Mark found his compartment, rushed inside, and was hardly aware of the cramped, antiseptic quarters, the single hard-looking hammock, the machine hovering over it, the sleep-thinker. He dropped, emotionally exhausted, to the hammock. With trembling fingers he fastened the straps, which allowed him some digital freedom—just enough to activate the machinery which would put him to sleep. Mark took a deep breath, wondered what it was like to sleep uninterrupted for a whole year (It was a little like dying, he had been told, but you dreamed a lot, thanks to the sleep-thinker), and touched the red button with his fingertip. A cone of dazzling light swooped down.

The music was syncopated and the voice wailed the blues:

Sagittarius!
Delirious!
He'll never come back...

Mark Channing was asleep an hour before the Operation Disaster starship left Earth for subspace and Purname.

CHAPTER TWO

...nightmares and learning.

...every cubic mile of deep space, not empty space, for no space is truly empty, a single hydrogen atom is being spontaneously created every mili-second. This keeps the universe going, growing, expanding. (Maybe monsters are out there: picture of a monster, many-fanged and sleep disturbing, created spontaneously like a hydrogen atom from void and darkness. Silent screaming like a vivid splash of the color red. Blood and horror.)

...main sequence stars. But if a star moves slowly through the gas clouds of space, and we do not know why this should be so except that some stars do move slowly, others rapidly (vision of stars rushing and flashing, others crawling and bumbling along)

...if a star moves slowly, it digs a wider tunnel through the gas of space, the gaseous material thus lifted from deep space falling into the star itself, adding over the eons to the star's bulk until it becomes enormous, bloated, dazzlingly bright, a supergiant. (Parade of supergiant stars: Deneb, Rigel, Canopus.) And the supergiant thus formed, a star many thousands of times brighter than Sol, is a rare and beautiful object, but a foredoomed one. (Death-beds and death-masks of supergiants, dirging the Milky Way Blues.)

...fifty billion years, for that is the life-expectancy of a main sequence star like Sol which, as the eons pass, will contract, grow hotter, whiter, become a white dwarf, then fade, a red dwarf; an ember, a cinder, a black dwarf, lightless, without heat, leading its family of dead planets through the eternal vaults of darkness. (Earth, dying. Earth, dead, Proud Earth. Gone its life, its teeming cities. Gone rain and seasons and warmth and the sounds of the world. A cosmic speck, but it means so much to man. Still, fifty billion years is a great time, even astrophysically, for the galaxy of which Sol is a member is not yet more than five billion years old.)

...supergiants perish cataclysmically. We call their final death throes supernovae. Such stellar explosions have been seen from Earth. (The Christmas Star. Vision of the Three Wise Men, following, following a sky-beacon at night, bright as the moon. Tycho's Star. The great supernova recorded by the Chinese in the eleventh century.) For a period of several Earth days, the light, heat and other radiation given off by a sundered supergiant—a supernova—equals that given off by all ten billion stars in this galaxy.

Purname's sun, soon after your arrival, will go supernova.

...white dwarf first, contracting but becoming dazzlingly bright. Soon the supergiant is reduced in size to almost planetary dimensions, as it caves in on itself because it has exhausted its hydrogen but continues to radiate fiercely. Transmutation of heavier elements. (The alchemist's stone of medieval sorcerers, lead to gold.) But such fusion, unlike hydrogen to helium (picture of a hydrogen bomb, heavy water to helium and a big blow) does not release great quantities of energy. It absorbs them. And grows fantastically massive until a cubic inch of its interior must weigh a billion tons.

...eons of time. Then, suddenly, time speeds up. The supergiant, now an unstable dwarf, emits much hard radiation into space, along with light and heat.

In the last stage, as with the Purnamese sun, the massiveness and absorption of energy suddenly reaches a critical point. The resulting explosion, flinging the hot central core of the collapsed supergiant into space, is the most awesome of cosmic spectacles and will, naturally, instantly vaporize any planets the star might possess.

(Purname, fifth of the name. For your people have moved outward in successive stages from the first planet to the fifth, as your sun's heat increased in the last stages of its catastrophic collapse. Purname, Earth's sister, with your seas and forests and the sounds and smells of life. Your oceans won't boil, Purname. Grim bubbling brine never touching sandy shores. In a snapping of cosmic fingers, before boiling or melting of your bedrock, Purname, you will be gone. Snuffed out in the greatest explosion the universe has ever seen or will ever see.)

Supernova!

...the Purnamese function of Operation Disaster. Strangely, the Purnamese were able to make the first three moves on their own. In great migration fleets they deserted their too-hot first planet for the second, then for the third, then for the fourth. But all the efforts of their culture, all the splendid creativity of a race equal to Earth's, went into this desperate undertaking. As a result, Purnamese culture deteriorated. Hardly more than savages now. (Drums and chants, he'll never come back, hot throb of a jungle pulse beat.) Operation Disaster, earth contingent, moved the Purnamese twenty years ago from their fourth to their fifth planet. (Deserted ghost of a fleet now, circling Purname, fifth of the name, like Saturn's ring. Empty ghost ships, waiting, waiting, to save the people who built you, beyond saving themselves. Barbaric. Worshipping the sun that soon will destroy them.)

...dangerously hot environment. Jungle rot and deserts and oceans uncomfortably warm...last minute arrival of Operation Disaster rescue ship...agents, specialists to activate Purname's waiting evacuation fleet, to put the Purnamese in suspension sleep until a new home can be found for them, to evacuate them in time, evacuate them before the big blow...

Supernova!

...wiped out, but for one man. Religious war again a possibility if...memory of Anson Channing, who played a deity. (Father whom I do not know! Father and a god for the Purnamese, you died so they might live, father, didn't you?)...Possibly they might have forgotten entirely...no longer civilized...in fear and superstitious dread...sun-worshippers, worshipping in fear, not love...

Nightmares and learning. Jungle rites and a dead man, head split open, familiar man, dead man, father of my dreams, Purname sun-god embodied. Screaming and chanting and the march on the aliens who have taken us in ships our patriarchs say we ourselves have built...no gods! alien lies! tricks! kill them!

Purname...

Two hundred million inhabitants...the safety factor, for the core of Purname's sun, gone supernova, will be flung into space at a speed of five million miles an hour. Flee with them or without them, but flee in time to save yourselves...another tragedy like the Channing affair...murder of five hundred Earthmen by extra-ter-restrial savages...close Operation Disaster Academy and put an end to mankind's most worthy interstellar efforts...must not happen.

Nightmares and learning—and the pan-humanity dream of the founders of Operation Disaster:

Fact. If a collapsed supergiant and another star form a binary system, and if the collapsed supergiant explodes, some of its material (containing the necessary transmutations into heavier elements of which a main sequence star is not composed) will remain behind and, after eons, become a planetary system for the stable star.

Fact. This has happened perhaps ten million times in the Milky Way Galaxy.

Fact. At least one in ten of these planetary births should have produced a planet similar to Earth. Purname, sister…

Fact. One million planets, scattered in a million stellar planetary systems in the galaxy, which can support life as we know it.

Fact. If a planet can support life, the biologists tell us, life probably will rise.

Fact. Darwin's natural selection. There are obvious advantages of walking upright and carrying the brain several feet off the ground, in a thick-walled cranium, and having binocular eyes and two arms and opposable thumbs. Mankind, then, is not unique.

Fact. Purname and a dozen other planets prove this. Some day, we'll find them all. That is our job, our dedication, our life. And some of them need our help. Desperately, like Purname. Operation Disaster was born and will do its work until the dream of pan-humanity becomes a possibility and a reality across the sixty thousand light years of the Milky Way galaxy.

Mark Channing slept and dreamed and learned and aspired.

And finally, awoke.

CHAPTER THREE

IN THE FORWARD observation lounge of the Operation Disaster starship, they said, "So that's Purname. Hard to believe it's going to be vaporized instantly in about a month. Why, it doesn't even look to be so hot: it's all covered with cloud."

And they said, "The intense heat causes faster water evaporation. It's hot all right. And so damned wet that leather begins to rot as soon as you expose it down there. At least, it did on the last expedition."

And they said, marveling over the fact that they had slept a year and, sleeping, learned, "I don't feel any older. Do I look any older? One year. One year out of my life."

And they made jokes about Rip Van Winkle and other long sleeps—snoozes, they said—in legend and story. They were generally gay, but it was a nervous gaiety as they watched cloud shrouded Purname sweep up at them from the blackness of space.

Mark Channing was there in the observation lounge, alone. He hardly thought of his isolation at all now: he had been lonely all his life and never even thought that if he'd undertaken any career but extra-terrestrial anthropologist he could have lived normally. There had never been any doubt, though: he would follow in his father's footsteps. And so he would be alone.

The starship rushed into Purname's soupy atmosphere and white tendrils of fog became thick gray banks of fog and soon nothing but the fog could be seen through the viewport. There was much drinking, but no music now. A mechanical voice called suddenly:

CAPTAIN MACCREADY IS NOW ENTERING THE LOUNGE.

The buzz of conversation faded and the lounge was completely silent when the door irised and Captain MacCready, a grizzled old space veteran and a giant of a man close to seven feet tall, who was in overall charge of the expedition and the crew, stalked into the lounge.

"I'm a spaceman," he boomed. "I'm no expert on extra-terrestrial anything—except space. So, now that we've come to Purname and are soon to make planetfall, you might wonder what my job is. I'll tell you. I'm a kind of safety officer. It's my job to get you all back to Earth alive, when your work is done. It's my job to see that nothing foolhardy is attempted."

Someone asked, "Is what the expedition did last time—foolhardy?"

"I think so," boomed MacCready promptly, "Hell, yes."

"They saved the Purnamese."

"And died themselves, fellow."

Mark said, "They didn't come out here to sight-see, Captain. They had a mission to accomplish, and is there any man who can say they didn't accomplish it?" Immediately, he was sorry he had spoken. A man in Mark Channing's position should never seek the center of the stage.

"You're Channing, aren't you?" the Captain demanded.

"Yes, sir."

"*His* son?"

"Yes, sir."

"I wouldn't talk, Channing. What your father did caused the death of every member of the expedition but one."

"What my father did saved two hundred million Purnamese from certain death!" Mark answered hotly.

MacCready said, "Well, I'm not an Operation Disaster Academy man. I haven't been trained to think that extra-terrestrial lives are more important than Earth lives. So, if what you said is what every specialist aboard my ship thinks, I still have a crew to consider. A crew of Earthmen, Mr. Channing."

Mark thought, Earthmen. Convicts. Lifers, mostly. And, to earn a life sentence in the twenty-second century you had to be a habitual criminal of the worst sort. A few dozen convict Earthmen, and two hundred million Purnamese men, women, and children, all as human as Earthmen.

Someone said that what Anson Channing's son said very definitely was not representative of what the rest of them thought. There was general agreement and, visibly, Captain MacCready relaxed. Then he said, "The reason I wanted to make my position clear is this. Just like the old days of terrestrial warfare, and I mean specifically during the target run of a big intercontinental bombing craft, when the bombardier took charge, the captain of the ship relinquishing control to him—so it has to be with us, by law. Your Operation Disaster Director, Dr. Culcross, will be taking over as soon as we land on Purname. Dr. Culcross knows the native ways, and I don't. Dr. Culcross is an expert, and I'm only an astrogator. But I wanted to make my point clear first. I wanted to show where my sympathies lie. Are there any questions?"

THERE WERE NONE. Mark was thinking. Then why? Why in space does he think he's taken us across two thousand light years? To turn tail at the first sign of trouble?

The expedition leader, Dr. Culcross, was introduced. He was a small, bent, scholarly-looking old man and Mark thought that MacCready purposely stood by his side to point up the contrast. Dr. Culcross spoke in vague terms of the expedition's mission, of the tradition behind the O.D. Agents, of the interstellar brotherhood of humanity, which was the dream of Operation Disaster. Then he got down to cases, saying, "An expedition of this sort, naturally, is made up of specialists in many fields. For a while, at least, most of you can take a holiday—aboard ship. Our first foray will be made by the extra-terrestrial anthropologists and sociologists, who have been given, by the sleep-thinker, a thorough knowledge of what Purnamese culture was like twenty years ago. They must now correlate this learning with the facts as they stand today. Meanwhile..." he chuckled, "I wouldn't be averse to the rest of you sleep suspension experts, astrogators, rocket engineers, and the like, throwing a ship-wide party. There'll be plenty for you to do later, if the anthropology people tell us it's safe." He paused, nodded his head and looked up to ask, wordlessly, if there were any questions. Again, there were none. With Captain MacCready he turned on his heel and went through the irising door.

And the microphone blared:

ANTHROPOLOGISTS AND SOCIOLOGISTS, FORWARD!

Mark's heart pounded up against his ribs as he made his way forward. His father had been an anthropologist specializing in the Purnamese sun-worshipping religion.

He was the same. He went forward now for final instructions with the half dozen other social scientists aboard the starship. He noticed without surprise that Susan Jamison was one of them—without surprise because her father, like Mark's, had been an anthropologist. She did not meet his eyes.

But on the catwalk leading forward, Otto Spade was waiting. He placed his heavy hand on Mark's shoulder and said quickly, in a soft voice which no one else heard, "Be careful, boy. Everyone on this ship, the convicts too, are watching you. You look too much like your old man, they say, you have his exact job you—be careful, Mark."

Mark challenged, "You never come out and say what you really think. But you were on Purname twenty years ago, weren't you? And you don't hate my father!"

"No, I don't."

"What he did was right. It had to be done, didn't it?"

Otto Spade did not answer, but his big fingers squeezed Mark's shoulder and Mark knew he was trying to be friendly.

Then Spade said, scowling, "It's incredible how like your father you are."

After that, Mark filed forward with the others to receive his final briefing before planetfall on Purname.

CHAPTER FOUR

THE FACE of the Sun had changed.

Not the sun in the sky, the sun that was rarely seen these days, obscured by thick clouds—but the sun atop the shrine in Purname City. The god-sun.

It was smaller, and brighter. The priests had made it that way, for hadn't the sky-sun itself, on the rare occasions when they saw it, become smaller and brighter?

The priests had coated the god-sun with darkness-glowing paint, and at night especially it was beautiful. At night also it was cooler and so they worshipped more frequently at night, but it was still chokingly hot even in the darkest, coolest hour of the night.

Mandit Karr, who was not a priest but a retired old warrior, often worshipped at night. Then, with the others of his faith—and on Purname a man either had the faith of the god-sun or no faith at all—Mandit Karr would climb the terraces of the shrine, singing a thousand-year-old chant at each level, his gnarled old arms reaching upward and out as if somehow he could grab the image of his deity there atop the shrine, gleaming and serene, and merge himself with it. And then, at such times, when the efficacy of his lord, the sun, really reached him, his thoughts would go back across the years to a time when he was still a warrior, and Captain of a Hundred, a time in his strong middle years, when the god-sun had come down to Purname.

He stared raptly at such times at the image of his deity, his eyes filling with water either from the fierce glow or with memory of what had happened. Ch'nanq had come down to his people. Ch'nanq! Wasn't it written that, in times of trouble, Ch'nanq would alight on Purname in the guise of a mortal, of a young man from the sun's own domain, the sky? And hadn't Ch'nanq come thus? He had come, Mandit Karr thought bitterly, and had been slain, along with his sky-host, so that only one minor follower of the deity escaped. And this, Mandit Karr thought chokingly, bitterly, bleakly, after Ch'nanq and his followers had removed all that was left of mankind from its burning world—the world was burning, doubtless, because Ch'nanq had not been worshipped properly, but Ch'nanq was a forgiving deity—and deposited them safely on Purname (fifth of the name) in vessels which they themselves had built and forgotten how to use!

Ch'nanq! Glorious god-sun! Master of the sky, forgiving Ch'nanq!

Ch'nanq! The air grows hot and it chokes and the rains flood us in the lowlands, Ch'nanq! Of winter we know nothing now, and the spring and fall are lost in the fierce blaze of summer, tempered only by the flooding storms of the heavenly waters, of your wrath, Ch'nanq! But is it not written that you will return to us, oh Ch'nanq? Return in our time of desperate troubles and vouchsafe us another chance for survival, that we might prosper and sing a paean to your name? is it not written so—Ch'nanq!

Mandit Karr hobbled on his one leg to the next terrace of the shrine. He had lost his right leg from above the knee during the fighting and the riots after the coming of Ch'nanq. The words still rang in his ear—terrible words. False god! they shouted in the streets and shrines of the new Purname City. False god! Bringer of ruin! Driver from homes! False god! And crying thus the crowds had formed in the streets of the new Purname City, and the soldiers, under Mandit Karr and others, had been powerless to stop them. Only one small spaceship, which had been within the belly of the bigger starship, had escaped. But its pilot had not been the god-sun Ch'nanq, for they had found the mortal shell of Ch'nanq's godhood, its head split from crown to jaw, its eyes open and staring and crawling with flies in the stifling heat.

But this, Mandit Karr told himself, had not been Ch'nanq. Ch'nanq—with flies crawling in his sightless eyes? Ch'nanq, indeed! Wrathfully, Ch'nanq had returned to his home in the sky, had retired in his wrath behind the great banks of clouds, and hardly showed his face to the people anymore, but only let them feel his withering heat. Still, and Mandit Karr smiled serenely as he reached the topmost terrace and bathed in the light of his deity, the fact that Ch'nanq had not destroyed the world meant that his righteous wrath would subside and that someday he would smile again on his people.

For they hadn't forsaken him, not entirely. The shrines were still worshipped at, and the old chants sung. Ch'nanq, thou glorious! We await your return in our time of troubles, Ch'nanq!

Slowly, on his one good leg and the peg, Mandit Karr began his descent on the other side of the shrine. Terrace by terrace he made his way down...pausing on each level to make his offering to the sun. The priests of the sun accepted his money, their claw-like hands jerking clear of the wide sleeves of their saffron robes, but he did not like the priests of the sun. It seemed incredible to him that the beliefs of a retired old soldier could be more in keeping with the traditions of their worship, but he knew it was so. And the priests, who did not really believe in Ch'nanq any more, not since the First Coming, accepted money in his name. But fortunately, Mandit Karr thought, there are others like myself…

There was yelling down below.

Mandit Karr's ears—not as sharp as they once had been—became aware of it only when he reached the fifth terrace. Figures were rushing about in the hot still darkness, shouting. A babble of confusion, with one sound repeated over and over again.

Ch'nanq!
Ch'nanq has come!

MANDIT KARR rushed to the final terrace, and from it to the ground. His heart was pounding, his limbs had become so weak they barely obeyed his whirling brain, and his breath was whistling in his throat. Ch'nanq!

Of course, he couldn't be sure. Whenever the name was mentioned, others hooted it down. And no, the crowd was not a jubilant throng awaiting the return of the deity. The crowd was loud, without humor, passionate and—not entirely unexpectedly, Mandit Karr had to admit—self-divided. There were some who rushed to the terraced shrine, attempting to tear down or at least deface the images. But others fought them off and sang the name of the god-sun. Blood flowed in the streets around the shrine even before Mandit Karr learned exactly what was happening.

"Fellow!" he said, collaring a stout sweating youth with his back to the first terrace of the shrine, defending it, "What has happened?"

"Ch'nanq!" wheezed the fat boy, and stuck his pudgy fist in another man's face.

"Ch'nanq, what?" Mandit Karr yelled.

"Has come again, some say," the fat boy told him, sweat streaming down his face as he lashed out with one thick leg and drove back a woman carrying a firebrand. "In the Field of Sorrow, friend. Where he died the last time. I believe. I believe!" the boy screamed devoutly, and died as someone down below jumped, caught his legs, and ripped his abdomen across with a bone-handled dagger.

Mandit Karr leaped from the low terrace, for the first time in his advanced years forgetting the fact that he was but one-legged. He stumbled and fell and instantly the crowd trampled over him and he was forced, face down, into the ooze and mud of a hundred violent rainstorms. He struggled, gasping, until he could fight clear and draw breath, dragging himself into a sitting position and shielding his head with crossed arms, then grasping an hysterical man's behind, and his middle, and his shoulders, to pull himself upright. He looked once at the terraced shrine, but the saffron-robed priests had fled, lacking the courage to fight on behalf of the god to whom their lives were supposedly dedicated.

Mandit Karr spat in disgust and fought his way toward the rear of the mob. His place was not here, fighting before the shrine. He loved the shrine, but if Ch'nanq had returned to the Field of Sorrow…

Wheezing and panting, Mandit Karr tore himself from the crowd's collective grasp.

"For Ch'nanq!" a voice screamed almost in his ear, and a big fist clobbered his face. Mandit Karr fell into the mud once more, and was kicked, and trod on. Then the berserk fellow found another foe and, dirty and battered, Mandit Karr stood on his one sound leg once more. I'm old, he thought.

Old age—a disease you did not recover from. Wearily, he dragged himself through the crowded streets toward the Field of Sorrow. He wondered if, before this night was over, blood would again be flowing like floodwaters through the streets of Purname City.

CHAPTER FIVE

THE FIELD of Sorrow was an enormous oval of greensward on the eastern edge of Purname City. It had been cleared and planted with the best grass seed of two worlds twenty years before, before the riots had started. It had not been called the Field of Sorrow then; it had been given that name later by the Purnamese after the people from the sky had been vanquished, as much because they would not fight back as because their weapons had failed them before the onslaught of ten million Purnamese who blamed them for the choking heat, and the floods, and the forced migration from Purname (fourth of the name).

In the very middle of the Field of Sorrow now, squatting there like some immense bug, was the starship. This was according to plan, for the Operation Disaster expedition of twenty years ago had laid out the field as a flat expanse to receive the ship of the next—and final—expedition. On it, the members of the expedition, first rescuing the false deity Anson Channing, who had almost succeeded in the role of Ch'nanq, Purnamese god-sun, had perished.

It was night and although no rain fell, rain was in the thick, soupy air. The field was muddy, but if it did not rain soon all the moisture would be wrung from the Field of Sorrow and the choking dust would make it difficult to breathe. On the edge of the greensward a crowd had gathered, and even from this distance you could hear their disturbed murmuring. Disturbed, not angry, for you couldn't tell yet what the noise meant...

"Purname," Mark Channing said.

Susan Jamison told him, "Get your feet back on the ground, Channing. You're only a man." Mocking him because his father had played a deity. But didn't she feel any of the wonder of it? of another world, a sister Earth, two thousand light years across galactic space? of a crumbling civilization, which owed its very existence to a handful of Earthmen who had perished that it might live?

Group Leader Hoffstaeder, an anthropologist who had been a student at the Academy when the last Purnamese expedition ended in disaster, raised his hang and instantly his companions stood still. "There's no sense just marching out there," he said. "The crowd sounds mean."

"Maybe they're just frightened, sir," Mark suggested. "After all, wouldn't you be if a deity had just come down?"

"We're not armed," Hoffstaeder said pointlessly.

"Who said anything about a deity?" Susan Jamison demanded. "My father's logbook clearly said that the expedition did everything it could to dispel that notion, even though Anson Channing had fabricated it without authorization."

"But don't you see?" Mark cried. "That's what caused all the trouble! They believed in my father. Faced with catastrophe and fast losing hold of whatever civilization and culture they had left, they needed something to believe in. Then, when the expedition decided to deny the god in their midst, the Purnamese broke into factions, and—"

"That's enough, Channing, Jamison." Hoffstaeder said. "We haven't come here to go over all the old issues again. We've come here to do a job and the first step is to see what sort of reception our technicians can expect. Which is why we social scientists were first out."

Mark asked, "Then what are we waiting for?"

"Channing, don't you understand anything?" Hoffstaeder snapped. "I never said I wasn't on your side—in theory. But we can't simply rush into this. We can't take the chance, because—"

"Are our few lives more important than two hundred million Purnamese facing certain death when their sun goes supernova?"

"*Will* you listen to me? Are two hundred million Purnamese worth the future and possible intergalactic brotherhood of all mankind?"

"No," Mark admitted, wondering what the Group Leader had in mind.

"All right. Then we can't afford to lose our lives here. The expedition must be a success—in every way. Do you think the Academy and everything it stands for could function without yearly national donations on Earth?"

"No, but—"

"And do you think those donations will be made if we perish like the last expedition perished—even if we succeed in getting the Purnamese into space?"

"I guess not, but—"

Wong, the linguist, said suddenly, "They're coming, Chief."

"A delegation?" asked Hoffstaeder, peering into the darkness. Liu Wong had the sharpest eyes among them.

"It does not look like a delegation," Wong said promptly, anxiously.

SOON THE others saw the crowd approaching them across the expanse of greensward. Those in the forefront were running, but not rapidly. Their feet made a sodden sound in the mud and the clinging ooze slowed them down. When they came closer it could be seen that they brandished sticks and clubs, but some behind them and fighting to gain the forefront were weaponless and shouted, "Ch'nanq! Ch'nanq!"

"Tell them we come in peace," Hoffstaeder told Wong uneasily. He knew that Captain MacCready's crew, watching from the viewports of the Operation Disaster starship, would back them with blasters if necessary. But if it turned out to be necessary then the expedition would end in abortive failure almost before its work had got underway.

Wong bellowed something in the Purnamese tongue, Mark, who had a fair grasp of Purnamese, heard him say: "It is necessary that we come to help you once more in your time of troubles, brothers of Purname."

But the Purnamese hooted him down and jabbered back at him and he turned to Hoffstaeder and said, "I'm afraid they won't listen, Chief."

Hoffstaeder shook his head wearily. "We couldn't tell in advance what their reaction would be. All right, then. We're going back to the ship."

"But we can't!" Mark cried. "We've got to—"

"We aren't through yet, Channing," Hoffstaeder said, "not by a long shot. We'll wait until the interest in the ship dies down, and send a couple of researchers out in secret, and—"

"Wait!" Mark exploded. "How can we wait? Every minute we wait makes it that much of a gamble with the lives of the Purnamese. Don't you understand, sir? This world is due to be vaporized. Vaporized, sir, in a split second. Besides, if we send researchers out in secret, and if they're found sneaking around, how would that look to the Purnamese? We've got to be forthright, and—"

"Like your father?" Susan Jamison said coldly.

"Yes, like my father. His name happened to sound like the name of their god. It wasn't his idea at first, you'll find that out if you bother to read *your* father's logbook carefully. And Lord knows no love was lost between our fathers. But he was honest. He never claimed to be a deity."

"He never denied it."

"He thought it better not to deny it."

The Purnamese by this time had formed a half circle around the Earthmen, waiting for them to make the first overt move. There was much shaking of clubs and rattling together of sticks, though. The Purnamese, all males, were dressed only in loincloths in the sultry heat. To Mark they looked neither savage nor civilized but in some intermediary stage. Finally, one of them spoke. He talked rapidly and there was competition from the others and even some fighting in the rear ranks of the two hundred or so natives, so Mark couldn't make out his words. But Wong translated faultlessly:

"Go back where you come from, skymen. A generation ago you caused the blood to flow like floodwaters in the streets of our city and already with news of your coming there are riots. Go back."

"Tell them," Hoffstaeder said, "we'll return to our ship but we're not leaving Purname, not just yet."

Wong spoke and was immediately answered. "They said we must leave Purname immediately. They repeated we cause disturbances and riots."

Hoffstaeder shook his head and muttered in English, "And can save all their lives, if they'll let us. Tell them no, we cannot go away. Tell them we are here to help them again."

Wong spoke, and fierce voices drowned out his words. "They threaten, Chief," Wong said. "I think we'd better go back, I think ..."

A stone was flung, striking Wong in the shoulder. He cried out in surprise and pain and would have stumbled and fallen, but Hoffstaeder caught and steadied him. "Retreat, men," he said. "Orderly. No rushing. And don't turn your backs."

They edged toward the starship. The Purnamese followed them, half a dozen darting forward, brandishing clubs and sticks and shouting. At first Mark remained in his tracks, not wishing to retreat with the others and admit even temporary failure so soon after they had left the ship. Hoffstaeder called him urgently while the vanguard of the mob drew up half a dozen strides from him, jabbering among themselves.

Then, suddenly, Susan came toward Mark, taunting, "Do you want to be left behind to play a god, as your father did?"

BEFORE MARK could answer, things happened very swiftly. Three of the Purnamese rushed between the rest of the expedition and Susan and Mark. The remaining three swooped down on Mark and the girl, yelling fiercely. One swung his stick and it whistled by over Mark's head. Mark displayed his hands, palm outward, to show he was unarmed, but the Purnamese swung again and the stick *thunked* against Mark's shoulder, spinning him around and dropping him. His arm ached clear down to the fingertips but he shook himself and climbed unsteadily to his feet.

Susan screamed. She struggled in the grasp of two of the natives, kicking and writhing, but they bore her off while the others stood their ground, Mark rushed at them and was driven to the ground again by a rain of blows. He collapsed in the hot smothering darkness, dimly aware of feet pounding and squashing across the muddy ground.

"They took Jamison," he heard Hoffstaeder say. Then he felt himself borne back toward the starship and a voice cried: "We've got to go after her." He did not realize it was his own voice and that no one paid any attention until after they were inside the ship and the airlock had closed behind them.

He never quite lost consciousness, but remembered vaguely being taken to the ship's infirmary, being examined by one of the medics, being given a hypodermic and some dressings for his bruises.

Then—he never knew how much time had elapsed—Dr. Culcross, the expedition's leader, was at his bedside. "I'm afraid you made a mess of things, son," he said.

Mark didn't answer. "Hoffstaeder tells me that if you'd gone back with the others, the girl wouldn't have been taken. But that's neither here nor there. Can you think straight? Can you answer some questions?"

Mark nodded, thinking of Susan Jamison. It was his fault, all right, for she'd come to get him, even if she had done so with a taunt on her lips.

"The consensus of opinion is that some religious fanatics took Jamison—possibly as a sacrifice to appease their god."

"But the Purnamese don't go in for human sacrifice!" Mark cried out.

"Didn't, you mean. Twenty years ago. Channing, don't you see, we're dealing with a people who have slid back a generation closer to savagery? But you're our expert on their religion, so we wanted to ask you—"

"How can I tell you anything, Dr. Culcross, if we're in basic disagreement? The whole concept of the Purnamese religion is opposed to the very idea of human sacrifice."

"*Was* opposed, you mean."

"All right. But if you've already convinced yourself, why ask me?"

"We're convinced of nothing. It was only a guess on the part of the other anthropologists, but don't you see, the girl's life may be in the balance? What we want to know is the sort of procedure the Purnamese could be expected to follow, where they might take their victim, how we might be able to find them…"

"You're going after her?" Mark asked hopefully. So far, everything about the expedition had been frustrating, because no positive action had been taken.

"I didn't say that. We must remember Captain MacCready's advice, Channing. But if we know what to expect, and if somehow we could get a message through, agreeing to leave Purname if they return Miss Jamison…"

"Leave? And let the Purnamese die in the supernova explosion?"

There was no answer to that.

Dr. Culcross looked at Hoffstaeder, who shrugged. Finally Mark nodded and told them he would sketch in the Purnamese sun-worshipping religion for them, and did so. His body ached from the blows he had received, but while he spoke he could feel his strength slowly returning. Just as he finished, a member of the crew rushed into the infirmary, saluted and shouted:

"A mob of the natives! Coming this way! Throwing things!"

HIS WORDS were hardly necessary, for just then a clattering hail of stones resounded against the ship's hull. The crewman's eyes were big with fright and Mark could imagine what he was thinking—how he'd signed on with the expedition to get out of the penitentiary for a while, but how he hadn't expected anything like this.

Dr. Culcross rushed into the companionway and Mark followed him. They found Captain MacCready near the main airlock, talking with some of the non-coms, the few non-convicts in the crew, including Otto Spade.

"...mow them down with blaster fire," the Captain was saying. "But we're not going to, with Dr. Culcross' permission; we'll leave this world first."

"But not without Miss Jamison," Dr. Culcross said.

Captain MacCready gave him a long, searching look. "I hope not," he said slowly, "I sincerely hope not, doctor. Naturally, though, we couldn't endanger the entire expedition for one person."

Almost, Mark found it hard to believe his ears. MacCready was no martinet. It might have been better if he were. No, he was firm but polite, co-operative, and could even be charming. But, Mark now realized, he was one of those military men incapable of filling a command position. He knew the letter of the military regulations, but would never understand the spirit if he lived to be a hundred.

"Mr. Spade tells us the crew is uneasy," he informed Dr. Culcross. "Isn't that right, Mr. Spade?"

"Yes, sir. The Cons are grumbling. But what the hell, cons always do."

"Anything serious?" Dr. Culcross asked.

Spade shrugged. "Never can tell, with cons. Give the non-coms half a chance to whip them back into a semblance of discipline, though, and you can forget your worrying."

"I don't follow you," Dr. Culcross said.

"Captain's orders, doc. Go easy on the crew."

Dr. Culcross' face whitened in anger as he looked at the military man. "Don't you realize if we lose discipline we've lost everything?"

"Doctor," recited Captain MacCready, "I was told to forget my crew was made up of convicts, I was told to treat them as free men."

"Well," said Otto Spade, "free men in a spaceship crew have got to take orders, Cap'n."

"I'll thank you to keep out of this!" MacCready snapped.

Culcross raised his eyebrows at Spade, but the big-chested, short-legged man shrugged. Just then a crewman rushed up and said, "Sir, someone's at the rear airlock!"

"Purnamese?"

"Yes, sir."

"Excuse me, gentlemen," Captain MacCready said, preparing to follow the man outside, stones continued to clatter against the ship's hull. Although they received no invitation, the other three followed Captain MacCready aft.

The Purnamese had been admitted to the airlock chamber, but the inner door was still secured. Half a dozen crew members were milling uneasily about it.

"Has any of you men a blaster?" the captain asked.

"We're not allowed to bear arms, sir," one of the crewmen reminded him as Otto Spade said: "I'm armed," and drew out his blaster.

"Open the inner door, then," Captain MacCready said.

Someone came forward and turned the lock-wheel and a moment later the tumblers clicked. Wong the linguist had been summoned and was just arriving when a tall, solemn-looking, tan-skinned Purnamese entered the ship. Twenty years ago, according to Hurley Jamison's logbook and the stories Otto Spade had told, the Purnamese were white-skinned, whiter than Caucasian Earthman. But now, if this man were any indication, a change in their sun's radiation had tanned them a rich bronze color.

THE PURNAMESE took two steps into the companionway, and fell forward, Mark lunged at him, catching him before he hit the floor. Blood welled suddenly from his mouth and nose, his shoulders and back were raw and welted. He had been clubbed almost to death.

"Get a doctor!" Otto Spade cried.

"Question him if you can," Captain MacCready told Wong.

For once Mark found himself in agreement with the Captain. If the Purnamese had come here to tell them something they had to hear it no matter what. Mark eased the native to the floor, took off his tunic and folded it for a pillow, then offered him water which someone had brought in a little flask. The man drank greedily, but could not hold the water down. It came up again mixed with blood.

"Lung damage," Captain MacCready guessed. "Maybe a rib's punctured it. Well, go ahead. Wong."

Wong spoke Purnamese slowly, earnestly. The native shook his head and Wong said, "He has nothing to do with the mob outside. When the mob saw he was trying to come in here, they beat him and stoned him."

"Then ask him what he does want," Captain MacCready said.

Wong spoke again. The native answered slowly, haltingly, the flow of blood from his mouth hardly more than a trickle except when he coughed. And Wong said:

"There seem to be two factions, sir. The group outside wants us to leave at once. The group this man represents is holding Susan Jamison as a hostage so that, should we stay, they can be assured we plan no harm for them."

Captain MacCready said, "Would a migration into space if we tell them their planet is doomed be considered a harmful act?"

Wong repeated the question and the Purnamese nodded at once, earnestly, then spoke. Wong translated, "He says their god does not tell them to move. He says they have no further place to go."

"Tell them we'll find a new world for them," Dr. Culcross said. "A better world. A permanent home for all their people. Tell this man that their world is doomed. Tell him we don't have much time in which to act. Tell him if we don't begin the evacuation soon, many will perish needlessly."

Wong spoke. Whenever he paused for breath, the native shook his head. Mark could understand most of the words although he didn't have Wong's facility for speaking them. Clearly, the injured native wasn't buying anything.

"If you do any of these things, captain," Wong said, "he assures us the girl will never be returned."

Captain MacCready shook his head bitterly. "They couldn't even return Miss Jamison if they wanted to, not with that mob out there. Ask him about that."

Wong put the question in Purnamese, but abruptly the native hemorrhaged, the blood gushing from his mouth and nostrils. The medic arrived moments later, but by then the Purnamese had lost consciousness. The medic was unable to stop the bleeding and the Purnamese died on the way to the infirmary.

Captain MacCready asked Wong, "Did he say anything about where they were keeping her?"

"No, sir. He did not."

"Wasn't there any indication?"

"Sir," Mark interrupted, "I consider myself responsible. I'd like permission to go after the girl."

"You? What could you do? You couldn't even get past that mob outside."

"If the native got in, I could get out."

"He got in—and died."

"I could try one of the other locks. Or I could get out through one of the exhaust vanes, they wouldn't be expecting that. I know I could make it, sir."

"Then what would you do?"

"Why, go to Purname City and find Miss Jamison and bring her back."

"Just like that, Channing? You're an anthropologist, not an expert on one-man guerilla warfare."

"But that's just it, sir! I'm an expert on Purname. I know this planet. I know Purname City. If anyone has a chance to get through and find Miss Jamison, I'm the man."

"What the lad says makes sense, sir," Otto Spade said.

But Captain MacCready shook his head.

"I'll go with him, sir," Otto Spade said unexpectedly.

Mark looked at the older man with surprise.

But Captain MacCready shook his head. "No, I'm afraid not. You wouldn't have a chance. Besides, Spade, I need you here, I appreciate the way you both volunteered to risk your necks, but the answer is no."

LATER, still feeling weak from his beating, Mark retired to his cabin. He felt utterly helpless and wondered what they were doing with Susan Jamison right now, this minute. The fact that she hated him because her father had hated his father hardly mattered. She was in trouble and it was his fault.

The ship was very quiet now. Even the natives outside had put at least a temporary stop to the rain of stones. It would be sunrise soon on Purname, Mark thought. He wasn't sleepy although he knew he needed rest. Sunrise. At sunrise his last chance to sneak away from the ship without being spotted by the natives outside would be gone. But Captain MacCready had turned him down.

Mark shook his head bleakly, wondering if it had gone this way twenty years ago. Had his father, also volunteering, been turned down? Perhaps, but his father hadn't stewed over it. His father had taken the bull by the horns and...

...And his memory was hated to this day. But still, what did that matter? Hated or not, his father had been responsible for the success of the last Operation Disaster mission to Purname, hadn't he? And I'm his son, Mark thought. No love is lost on me because they don't think I merit being an Agent. Well, if I have the name, I might as well have the game...

Mark got up quickly and slipped out into the companionway. He took three strides in the dim blue nightlit companionway—and collided with someone.

"Mark?" a rasping voice said softly.

"Otto! I thought—"

"I guess we both had the same idea, boy. I was coming to get you. If that captain thinks we're going to let them keep the girl without making a move—but mind you! No tricks like your old man pulled, or I'll take you over my knee and tan your hide. And don't think I couldn't do it, either. Well?"

Mark stuck out his hand, wordless, and Spade shook it.

"Exhaust vane?" Mark asked quietly.

"I think so. They wouldn't expect that outside. We'll come out covered with grease, but we'll come out without being spotted. Let's go."

Fifteen minutes later, they had carefully jimmied loose the vane's inner cover. Inside it smelled of grease and spent air and ozone. Mark went first, crawling awkwardly, slipping on the greased surface, then stretching out full length and crawling when he approached the narrow rear of the tube, barely wide enough to admit him.

When he reached the end, Mark struck his head against something solid. He could hear Spade's grunts as the older man worked his way through the tube behind him. Mark said, "Lid's on, Otto."

"Probably covered it to keep out the dampness. Wouldn't want one of these babies to go rusty on you. Try and force it, boy."

Mark stretched his hands out and pushed. He could not get the strength of his shoulders behind them, though, and the lid did not yield an inch.

"Don't push on her steadily," Spade said. "She has to be jerked loose. Give her some blows with your fists, boy."

Mark struck the lid repeatedly with both fists, pushing his arms straight forward and not getting his weight behind them. The lid remained secure.

"I can't budge it."

"Keep trying."

Mark pounded at the lid again, wondering suddenly if the Purnamese natives outside would hear the sound and be able to locate it. Then, all at once, although his last blows seemed no harder than any of the others, the lid came loose. The air was clean and fresh—but, incredibly, even hotter than the close air inside the exhaust vane, Mark squirmed out of the vane and shinned himself down to the ground. The effort it took was only slight, but covered him with sweat.

A moment later, Spade came down heavily alongside him. Spade was panting hard. "Hardly could breathe in there," he grunted, "and it isn't much better out here. Set, boy?"

"Set," Mark said.

"Then let's go."

Other shadows prowled about the darkness. Mark could see them, and knew they were Purnamese natives standing guard on the starship, perhaps intending to resume their fusillade in the morning. Crouching, trying to keep himself out of silhouette against the vaguely brighter sky, Mark headed across the wide, treeless field. He was aware of Spade dogging his footsteps and soon broke into a jog.

Then Spade tripped.

He sprawled heavily, crying out instinctively. A voice called out loudly in Purnamese, "Stop!" Spade picked himself up and hissed, "Quick…run for it! We've got to run for it."

Mark sprinted across the field. Shadows flitted before him, came closer, danced around him. He struck at the darkness with his fist and heard a scream. Something struck the ground, making a squashy sound. Muddy water splashed up at him and for a moment the ring of shadows was broken.

"Otto?" he called.

"Behind you!"

Mark ran.

CHAPTER SIX

MANDIT KARR still could not believe that the saffronrobed priests of Ch'nanq, had kidnapped the Earth girl and were holding her as a hostage. But it was so. It was so—and much else had transpired this night in Purname City.

Riots were widespread now. There were three factions: those who wanted to destroy the skyship; those who wanted the skyship to leave them in peace; and those, Mandit Karr among them, who believed Ch'nanq was returning to his people in their grave time of troubles. The priests of Ch'nanq belonged to the second group. They meant the girl no harm, they said, and Mandit Karr believed them. But with the girl in their hands, they said, the men from Earth would do nothing to which they were opposed.

Meanwhile, looters and rioters prowled the streets of Purname City. The priests had called upon Mandit Karr, a famous old military hero, for help. And, pegleg or no, Mandit Karr now found himself back in uniform.

He was in conference with Bah-Ch'nanq, the high priest of Ch'nanq, a withered old man with a black maw of a mouth and the longest fingernails Mandit Karr had ever seen and a smell like an old goat. Bah-Ch'nanq said in his reedy voice.

"First, the riots must be stopped. We control nothing if we do not control our own people."

"But," Mandit Karr protested, "what about the Earth ship? What about—"

"Ah, then you do call it an Earth ship? Merely a ship from another world, a sister world to Purname? I thought you believed that sacrilege of the deity returning…"

"And still you put me back in uniform?"

"We need you, Mandit Karr. The people know your name. They trust you. What you believe does not matter for the moment."

"I have not changed my beliefs."

"You truly think Ch'nanqs in that ship, returning to us?"

"Yes," said Mandit Karr devoutly.

The high priest Bah-Ch'nanq grinned his toothless, black-mawed grin, "A god—in a spaceship?"

Mandit Karr shrugged. "I do not know how gods travel between the worlds, Bah-Ch'nanq. I only know that last time Ch'nanq came to—"

"If it was Ch'nanq."

Mandit Karr laughed softly. "I believe you are afraid to face the personification of the god whose godhood it is your business to worship."

"Look you, Mandit Karr," Bah-Ch'nanq said. "If that had indeed been the lord Ch'nanq a generation ago, think you he could not have saved our world?"

"He chose another way."

"Evacuating us from a world which could no longer support us! For it had grown too hot—with the heat of Ch'nanq the sun, Mandit Karr. Mark you this. His own heat. Yet, instead of stopping it, he came to us and—"

"I don't know the ways of the god."

"But you believe?"

"I believe, Bah-Ch'nanq. Do you?"

The high priest's face, in color a paler version of the saffron yellow of his robe, drained pale. "Enough," he said. "You have your job, Mandit Karr. Your command awaits you. Stop the riots."

"Killing people who are as confused as I am—or as you are—is that what you want? Is that what Ch'nanq would want?"

"You have your orders. Control must be re-established or the city will fall to chaos."

Probably, Mandit Karr had to admit, the old priest was right at least about this. He asked, "The girl is safe?"

"Safe, yes. She's no concern of yours."

"Have you asked her if she's a handmaiden of the god?"

"Mandit Karr. Leave religious matters to me."

"But don't you see? The god's wrath—"

"I'll worry about the god's wrath. You worry about the rioters. They are thickest on the edge of the city, near the Field of Sorrow. My agents tell me that in the morning they will march, but it is not known where they will march. Either out to the Field of Sorrow and the Earth spaceship—or back here to the heart of the city and the shrine of Ch'nanq." Bah-Ch'nanq's small eyes grew crafty. "I tell you this, Mandit Karr. If they march on the spaceship, let them. Either the Earthmen will defend themselves, slaying many of the rioters and restoring order for us, or the mob will destroy the spaceship and expend its fury there on the Field of Sorrow. Mark you these words, then: if the mob marches onto the Field, let them go. Bar their return with your troops, if necessary."

Mandit Karr was stunned to silence. The high priest went on, "If, on the other hand, they march back toward the center of the city, and this shrine, then they must be stopped at all costs. Is that clear?"

It was clear, all right. Mandit Karr let the nails of his fingers dig in to his palms painfully. He had an impulse to throttle the high priest, whose first concern was for his own life. The veins on his neck stood out and with an effort he said.

"If the Bah-Ch'nanq's finished?"

"Yes, Mandit Karr. Execute the orders I have given you."

Mandit Karr bowed out of the audience chamber. He went outside to where his hundred handpicked troops were waiting. One hundred men—it hardly seemed like much in the teeth of a citywide riot. But, cursing softly and steadily, Mandit Karr issued his orders.

HE LED his troops from the courtyard of the shrine toward the Field of Sorrow. Dawn was already chasing the stars from the eastern sky, but torches and bonfires glowed red in Purname City. The soldiers were pelted with offal and stones and house-slops, but Mandit Karr refused them permission to retaliate. There was much derisive shouting, much threatening on all sides, but the band of a hundred men marched steadily in a compact formation across the city.

Here and there a fire-gutted ruin, still smoldering, bore testimony to the mob's violence. Bands of urchins roved too, looting. It seemed to Mandit Karr that all his people had needed was a spark to ignite them—and the spark had been supplied by the coming of the Earth ship.

Ch'nanq! he thought. We of Purname need you, if ever a people needed their god. Ch'nanq! Manifest yourself to us, Ch'nanq!

The mobs were larger and better organized on the edge of the Field of Sorrow. This would be so, Mandit Karr thought: they represented the faction which wanted to destroy the Earth ship. Mandit Karr called his troops to a halt, realizing that the strung-out marching formation would be dangerous here, for his men might be snipped off in groups as a shears snips cloth. Mandit Karr wheeled his hundred troops into a block-like battle formation ten across and ten deep, with a slight avenue bisecting the block from front to rear. The first line of ten was composed of lancers, their long pikes bristling, gleaming in the torchlight, forming a barrier protruding ten feet ahead of the massive formation. Behind the lancers stood two rows of bowmen and behind them, with swords and clubs, seven rows of foot soldiers, ready to break formation and charge up the avenue provided for them at Mandit Karr's command.

"Men!" Mandit Karr shouted, trying to mask his reluctance with the volume of his voice. "Here we stand! If the mobs come back from the skyship, we stop them. If they come from the rear, approaching the skyship, we open the foot-soldiers' avenue and let them pass and close behind them, barring return."

These were Bah-Ch'nanq's orders, and Mandit Karr gave them now to the soldiers of his command. But he prayed that something would happen which would make him disregard those orders. His soldiers were hand-picked, he knew: probably the best troops on all Purname. At first he had thought they could do little in the face of city-wide rioting, but now he wasn't so sure. Their formation was tight; their morale, excellent; their battle-readiness, superb. And, if Mandit Karr were given half an opportunity, they would be fighting on the side of Ch'nanq, though where the god's side lay was not as yet clear to the one-legged veteran.

A scout returned across the Field of Sorrow on the dead run, raised his arm in salute and cried, "They're coming this way!"

"Who, man?" demanded Mandit Karr.

"Rioters, sir. Chasing two from the skyship."

Mandit Karr bawled: "Formation—*read-iii!*"

Lances came up, were thrust back against rests, pointed forward in a solid line at an angle of thirty degrees. Bowmen notched arrows, waiting the order to draw them back. Foot soldiers drew their swords.

The pound-suck, pound-suck, pound-suck of feet running across the mud was heard and the angry challenge and counter-challenge of voices further out across the Field of Sorrow. In the first light of dawn Mandit Karr saw two figures rushing toward him, and a mob brandishing clubs and staves a half hundred paces back. The two fugitives were wearing the leatheroid jumpers of the Earthship people, and Mandit Karr's heart leaped into his throat as the sight of them dissolved twenty years of time.

"Open the footsoldiers' avenue!" roared Mandit Karr as the two Earthmen came staggering toward them through the mud. The Earthmen, seeing the battle formation materialize suddenly from the mists on the edge of the Field of Sorrow, tried to check their headlong flight and swerve off to one side. But momentum and the clinging mud made this difficult and another moment found them within Mandit Karr's formation.

"Lancers, for-*ward!*" yelled Mandit Karr, and his column of lancers advanced slowly on the van of the mob. Staves and lances rang together in the dissipating pre-dawn mists, shouts rolled out across the Field of Sorrow, and the mob—its energies spent in the long chase—was quickly scattered.

The lancers returned, sweating and elated. Mandit Karr spun about and stalked into the foot soldiers' avenue to see what game he had snared. The first Earthman, panting, grease-and-mud covered, glaring defiantly, was short, stocky, and seemed very strong. The second Earthman...

All at once Mandit Karr fell on his knees, touching his forehead to the soft, yielding ground, then lifting his eyes boldly for a second look which was immediately followed by a second prostration.

"The lord god-sun Ch'nanq has returned!" he cried in a voice which carried to all his troops.

Those nearest the Earthmen looked, and the older ones among them remembered the god Ch'nanq of twenty years before, if, indeed, it had been their deity.

The face they saw before them was the same.

Some of them had seen Ch'nanq apparently die, as Mandit Karr had. Did they need any further proof? Here he was again, reborn after a generation, returned to Pur-name to help them a second time. A man, a mere mortal, hacked to pieces before your very eyes by the blows of a dozen swords, could not return to life twenty years later. But a god could. A god could do anything.

"The lord god-sun Ch'nanq has returned!" Mandit Karr cried devoutly a second time.

Slowly, by two's and three's, the soldiers knelt before Mark Channing.

CHAPTER SEVEN

HERBERT FULLER, the chief astrogator of the Operation Disaster starship, destroyed the carefully plotted return-orbit a moment before the mutineers broke into the ship's astrodome.

The act was purely instinctive on Herbert Fuller's part. He did not have time to sit down and think it out carefully, step by step. Step one: fearing for their lives because the angry mobs outside the starship renewed their stoning in the morning and even brought a felled tree as a battering ram to use against the main airlock, the convict-crew broke into the arsenal, armed itself, and rushed swiftly to overpower the unarmed and outnumbered expedition members. Step two: the many little battles, most of which Herbert Fuller had not seen, all of which had been won by the mutineering crew resulting in six fatalities including the chief anthropologist, Hoffstaeder, ended in complete victory for the crew. Step three: a delegation came swiftly to the astrodome to secure the ship's return-flight orbit, realizing they could never leave Purname's solar system without it since sub-space orbits had to be calculated with almost awesome accuracy. Step four: Herbert Fuller had entered the astrodome seconds before they arrived, had rushed to his computing table and set a match to his calculations. Then the half dozen crewmen broke in.

"Give it to us," one of them said. There was a smear of blood on his forehead and probably, Herbert Fuller thought, it was not his own blood. Herbert Fuller was dazed by it all, still not precisely aware of what had happened. He had no way of knowing that half—if not more—of history's heroes are forged in just such confusion.

"No," he said, dropping the ash of the return-orbit to the floor.

"You burned it?" one of the crewmen asked.

Herbert Fuller nodded, stirring the ashes with the toe of his shoe.

"Compute it again," the leader of the crewmen ordered.

"No, I won't," Herbert Fuller heard himself saying.

"You better, son."

"I've had no orders from the captain."

"The captain's a prisoner."

"Then I'll have to make my own judgment," said Herbert Fuller. "The Jamison girl is still out there somewhere. And two members of the expedition were found to be missing this morning, making three in all out there. So—"

"He talks too much. Hit him."

The fist struck Herbert Fuller's jaw. He was a civilized man from a civilized world in a civilized job. He had never been struck before, not since he was a child. He had expected pain, but felt very little. What he felt was mostly a numbness flooding out from his jaw, engulfing him. Then he fell over backwards and his legs went up into the air foolishly and after that he lay on the floor.

"Compute another orbit," one of the crewmen said.

Herbert Fuller shook his head. Something tickled his chin and he rubbed at it with his hand and then looked at his hand, which now was glistening with blood, his blood, leaking from his mouth across his chin. It startled him.

Someone kicked Herbert Fuller's ribs, and that hurt more than the blow on the jaw. He groaned.

"If you have some crazy idea we're going to sit around," one of the crewmen said, "and let the natives break in here and kill us or maybe eat us—"

"They couldn't break in," said Herbert Fuller coldly, fighting down the nausea which had engulfed him as the numbness had engulfed him before. "Besides, the Purnamese don't eat people."

"Just compute the orbit."

"I will not do it," Herbert Fuller said.

THEY DRAGGED him to his feet. They hit him. They held him there when he would have fallen and hit him again. He was rocking back and forth. That was when they hit him and let him go and caught him. The pain wasn't very much. Then they hit him in the stomach and he collapsed slowly, wishing he could vomit but wishing he could begin breathing again first. After a while they threw water on him and dragged him to his feet again, and the talk went like this:

"Compute the orbit!"

"I will not compute it."

"We're going to hurt you some more."

"I will not compute it."

"Don't be a fool. What does it get you?"

"I will not compute it."

"Hit him, Stan."

"I will not…"

He was hardly aware of saying the words. Nor was he particularly aware of being struck again, of being supported from behind, of being doused with water a second time, and interrogated, and hit again, and doused, and bloodied…

Then he was unconscious.

"We'll kill him."

"You better not kill him. You want to be stuck here forever?"

"He must be made out of iron, look at him. Just a little guy. Without muscles."

"See if you can make him come to."

"No. He's really out. When he fell he hit his head pretty hard."

"Lift his eyelid and see if he's faking."

"Hey, will you look at that! The whites rolled back on him."

"Feel his heart, you fool!"

"O.K., but…"

"It's beating?"

"No. No, he's dead."

They crowded around Herbert Fuller's body, two or three of them taking turns examining him. None of them could discern a heartbeat. They did not look at the back of the dead man's head, which had struck a sharp flange of metal on the way down and which had been crushed.

Half an hour later, a delegation informed the imprisoned Captain MacCready that the starship's astrogator was among the casualties. "You fools," said Captain MacCready. "To return to Earth you stage a mutiny, and seven men die. How can you return to Earth now?"

The crewmen looked at one another, and most of them were smiling. They had not received life sentences in the penitentiary for petty larceny. "You're forgetting, captain," one of them said. They had no discipline, no acknowledged leader. They spoke when they had a mind to speak.

"You sure are forgetting," another one of them said.

"Well, what is it?"

"We're all lifers. There's no death penalty anyplace but on Earth. We go back to Earth—and we're right back where we started from. They can't do a thing to us they didn't plan to do already. Or—" a sudden light came into the old man's eyes—"how does this sound, men? We don't go back to Earth at all. We find ourselves a world somewhere, what we can live on. It's bound to be better than prison."

There was general assent, but Captain MacCready was laughing softly, steadily.

"What's so funny?"

"What you told me before. The astrogator was dead. You can't leave a planetary system for subspace without a carefully computed orbit, you know that."

"Sure, but don't try and tell us there ain't another astrogator on the ship's list! Leave Earth with one astrogator—like hell!"

"Oh, we have a pinch-hitting astrogator aboard," Captain MacCready said. "That is, we *had* one."

"What the hell do you mean by that, Cap'n?"

"Otto Spade," Captain MacCready said.

"Then get him."

Captain MacCready said, "Otto left the ship with Mark Channing sometime during the night. There isn't a living man aboard now who can plot a decent sub-space orbit."

The mutineers looked at one another in baffled silence. Nobody tried to stop him when Captain MacCready began his soft chuckling again.

CHAPTER EIGHT

"GET ON your feet," Mark said awkwardly in Pur-namese. "I'm not the lord god-sun. Channing is my name, and—"

"Ch'nanq!" cried the leader of the soldiers, the gnarled but powerful-looking one-legged man. "Ch'nanq is your name, sire. But did you have to tell us? Do you think we have forgotten? Think you we cannot see your identity written all over your face? Think you Mandit Karr forgets his lord?"

"Careful," Otto Spade grumbled. "It's happening just like it happened with your old man," Spade had spoken in English.

Turning to him, the one-legged soldier who called himself Mandit Karr said, "What does the lord's subaltern wish?"

"Lord's subaltern!" scoffed Otto Spade.

"But is it strange? I remember the lord's subaltern from his last visitation, a generation ago. It is all the proof we need of the god-sun's divinity."

"I don't get that," Spade told Mark, who shrugged.

"You see, lord," Mandit Karr went on, addressing Mark, "if for reasons of your own you chose to hide your identity, the fact that the subaltern of the lord has aged in these twenty years but that you remain precisely as we remembered you, is proof enough of your godhood. What do you wish of us, lord?"

Mark checked himself. The expedition—could the expedition do any better than he? But the expedition had all but admitted failure: Captain MacCready was for orbiting back to Earth and Dr. Culcross had been opposed primarily because Susan Jamison was a captive of the Purnamese. And, as a mortal member of the expedition, Mark knew he would fare no better. But as the deity of the Purnamese…

He smiled with grim amusement. He could almost imagine his father, twenty years before, faced with virtually the identical problem. Actually, Mark thought, he would find the path to godhood simpler than his father had, for Anson Channing had already paved the way and the remarkable resemblance between father and son did all Mark's speaking for him.

But if he dared the impersonation, the expedition would not back him.

On the other hand, if he didn't go through with it, the expedition would return to Earth in a short time and the doom of millions of Purnamese would be sealed. And besides, Susan Jamison was here in Purname City somewhere, and a god could find her a lot more swiftly than a mere mortal…

Mandit Karr was saying, "Has the Lord Jimson returned to Purname as well?"

"The Lord Jimson?" Mark asked.

"Surely I need not remind the Lord Ch'nanq of the Lord Hul-Jimson, who led the revolt of the gods which divided my people as it divided the gods and led to the physical death of the Lord Ch'nanq's previous visitation, as well as of the Lord Jimson and all their servants, except for the subaltern of the god, this man here."

The Lord Hul-Jimson thought Mark wildly. Wasn't that obviously Hurley Jamison, whose logbook, brought back as the only written record of the ill-fated previous mercy expedition, had been instrumental in condemning Anson

Channing's memory? Had Jamison, then, allotted to himself the role of a usurping deity? And had the Purnamese preferred their own Channing (Ch'nanq), angering the Lord Hul-Jimson? Could it be possible that Jamison, embittered for a reason they would never know, had turned both the expedition and some of the natives against the elder Channing? After all, Hurley Jamison had been the expedition's anthropological chief, and perhaps he'd been the sort of man who would resent the way Anson Channing had stolen his thunder. Naturally, such resentment wouldn't actively take the form it ultimately had taken, but that hadn't been something Jamison could control.

"No," Mark said slowly, deliberately, "the lord Hul-Jimson did not return. The Lord Hul-Jimson can never return, for the Lord Hul-Jimson was a false god."

"Mark!" warned Otto Spade.

"Sire," breathed Mandit Karr, kneeling once more. "I had always hoped it would be so. Then in the home of the gods, you won?"

Mark nodded solemnly, and said, "Is there news of a hand-maiden who—"

"The priests of Ch'nanq have her!" Mandit Karr groaned, "It hurts my heart to tell you, sire. Your own priests. The priests of Ch'nanq."

"In Purname City?"

"Yes, sire."

"Then take me there," Mark ordered.

"A moment, sire. How shall I say it...? The priests of Ch'nanq would rather worship idols than the return of their godhead. Sire, don't you see—they can control the idols."

"Then take me there," Mark said again.

Otto Spade grabbed his arm and said savagely in English, "Don't be a fool, lad. They're bound to be divided in the city. They'll tear you apart."

But Mark shook his head stubbornly. "They have Susan Jamison, Otto. It was my fault." He turned to Mandit Karr and cried over the din: "To Purname City!"

A moment later the military formation swept about and stormed across the edge of the Field of Sorrow toward the heart of Purname City and the rioting.

CHAPTER NINE

HE WAS a horrible looking old man and he smelled. It was an unclean smell, Susan Jamison thought, as the man himself was unclean. A dirty old man in a saffron yellow robe, chanting incantations in a small chamber hewn from stone at the top of the tower of Ch'nanq. He crouched before a fire and made passes over the flames with husk-like hands. It was almost as if he'd forgotten Susan Jamison was here, but she knew—the knowledge making her afraid—this wasn't so.

A stone door rolled ponderously open. Three saffron robed lesser priests entered the chamber and one of them spoke to the old man so rapidly in Purnamese that Susan could not understand what was said outside, the noise of the mobs roving the streets sounded far away, like the distant ebbing and flowing of surf.

The old man scowled and shouted something. The lesser priests cowered before him. Spittle dribbled across his chin. *He's mad*, Susan thought desperately.

Bah-Ch'nanq said slowly: "The false god returns. You knew that, didn't you?"

Susan shook her head slowly. She did not understand.

The old priest clutched at her arm. He was surprisingly, incredibly strong. He forced her back close to the fire until she could feel its hot breath on her legs. "You knew he would come!" the priest repeated.

"I—didn't—know—anything!" Susan sobbed.

One of the lesser priests jabbered again and Bah-Ch'nanq listened, his eyes narrowing to slits. "We still have the girl," Bah-Ch'nanq said when the lesser priest had finished. He had not let go of Susan's arm. When she tried to break from his grasp he struck her with his free hand and she whimpered and almost fell into the fire.

"What are you going to do with me?" she said.

"Is there a god on your skyship?" Bah-Ch'nanq asked.

"N-no."

"One who claims to be a god has returned here to Purname City a second time. Our people protested the coming of the skyship and rioted. But they won't fight their god."

"Ch—Ch'nanq?" Susan asked incredulously, thinking that Mark Channing wouldn't dare.

"Yes. The false Ch'nanq. Doubtless he will insist that we leave our planet again, as he did a generation ago. Well," Bah-Ch'nanq said, "perhaps all is not lost. Perhaps the other god has returned as well. Perhaps this time the other god will win."

"The—other god?"

"Hul-Jimson," said Bah-Ch'nanq reverently. "Last time, when the false Ch'nanq came to Purname, the unknown god Hul-Jimson came also. They fought and their fighting spread to my people. In the end, the false Ch'nanq had his way and we embarked for this world in the great fleet. But the men from the sky perished—to a man."

"Except one," Susan said dully.

"One?"

"One got away."

"True. True, the subaltern of the false god. With him he took the words of the god Hul-Jimson. He…"

THE PRIEST droned on, but Susan no longer heard him. She felt completely empty inside, shattered. Hul-Jimson. That, of course, would be Hurley Jamison. Her father. All her life she had idolized the memory of her father, always contrasting it with what she knew of Anson Channing. Somehow the image of her father had been good and pure and that of Channing, wicked. Channing, who had played god to a primitive people. And now Susan knew the truth: her father had done the same. In a sense, he had done worse than Anson Channing: for Channing had been mistaken for a deity by the Purnamese and had not bothered to deny it. But Hurley Jamison, if she could believe the dirty old man, the priest of Ch'nanq, had invented his own supernatural status.

A choice, Susan thought, the tears filling her eyes. Either my father was as wrong as Anson Channing and I have been guilty of the grossest injustice toward a dead man and his living son, or both Channing and my father did the only thing they could a generation ago—and in that case my injustice is even worse.

There was a third possibility but she refused to consider it. Anson Channing had played god because he had to. Hurley Jamison had played god because he had wanted to. Therefore, while Channing's godhood evacuated Purname (fourth of the name) and saved the Purnamese from fiery destruction, her father's godhood had caused dissention among the Purnamese—and the death of the Earth expedition.

"What are you going to do?" Susan asked the priest suddenly. She did not want to think about it now. She had to think of other things.

"They are storming the city," Bah-Ch'nanq said, "almost bloodlessly. On every street they gain a thousand converts. Such is the foolish faith of my people."

"Then there's nothing you can do about it?" Susan Jamison asked. She was almost happy, and it surprised her.

She realized now that Anson Channing's way, a generation ago, had been the only way. She thanked God that his son was here and able to follow in his footsteps.

Bah-Ch'nanq opened his black maw of a mouth, Susan realized he was smiling. "I wouldn't say that," he said. "I wouldn't say there is nothing we can do about it. We have you."

The lesser priests grinned. Susan looked at Bah-Ch'nanq's face, at the wild eyes, the drooling lips. This was a nightmare. It had to be a nightmare.

"If necessary," said Bah-Ch'nanq slowly, "we can dismember you limb from limb. First the small finger from each hand. Then the next finger. Then...but I'm sure you see. If the false Ch'nanq was kept informed of our progress, was perhaps shown the fruits of it, don't you believe he might be induced to leave us in peace?"

"You're mad!" Susan cried, rushing for the door after wrenching free of the old man's grasp. "You're a madman!"

One of the lesser priests barred her path, but she pushed at him and he became tangled in the swirling folds of his robe. Susan lunged for the door.

Which closed ponderously in her face with a jarring thud of stone on stone.

"Bring her here," said Bah-Ch'nanq slowly.

Susan screamed as the lesser priests came for her. But she knew no one outside the little room would hear her.

"CH'NANQ!" THEY roared on the street corners of Purname City as the full light of dawn and the day's first fierce heat engulfed the city.

"Ch'nanq!"

"Ch'nanq!"

The one word, torn from a thousand throats, became a surging sea of sound. The soldiers of Mandit Karr were surrounded and borne through the streets by the mob like conquering heroes. Spontaneous demonstrations of faith replaced the night's ugly rioting magically wherever they went. *This isn't for me,* Mark thought with deep emotion. It was for his father. It was wonderful, and the hour of it which Mark experienced made up for twenty years of pain.

They rolled with the crowd to the very center of Purname City, where the great Tower of the God pierced the heat haze flickering in the sky; Mark felt himself borne aloft on shoulders, carried about, lifted, dropped, lifted again, on a wild sea of humanity. He smiled. A god—or a conquering hero. The Purnamese hardly seemed to make the distinction.

There was talk nearby but he could not hear it in the noise the crowd made. Finally, long after he had reached the center of the city and when the sun had already risen high, radiating a searing, strength-sapping heat, several people dragged him to one side, Otto Spade and Mandit Karr among them.

"My people will do whatever you wish," Mandit Karr said. But strangely, his voice was sad.

"Then what's the matter?" Mark asked.

"The girl—the handmaiden of whom you spoke, Bah-Ch'nanq and the lesser priests have her. I remember the humanity of the Lord Ch'nanq last time—and I am afraid."

"What are you afraid of?" Mark said. "Tell them to release her! Tell them—tell them their god demands this."

"They worship only idols, sire. They will not listen."

"What are they going to do?"

"They threaten torture and death, sire—if you don't go away, I am a soldier but I am afraid. I know you won't let them have their way with the girl but..."

"Listen," Mark said. "Can we get up there?"

"Even if you tell them to," Mandit Karr groaned, "my soldiers wouldn't violate the shrine of the god."

"But think, man!" Otto Spade bellowed. "Here is the god, telling them..." It was an about-face for the burly crewman, but Mark knew it wouldn't do any good.

"And start what started a generation ago all over again?" Mandit Karr asked. "Civil war, strife..."

"All right," Mark said. "Your men won't go up there, Mandit Karr. Will you?"

"I go wherever the lord Ch'nanq leads."

"You're a dead man if you set foot on that ramp!" Otto Spade bellowed. "According to Mandit Karr the priests are in a small room at the top of the tower. They can look down and see every inch of that ramp. You wouldn't have a chance."

"There is truth in what the subaltern of the god says," Mandit Karr admitted. "However," he added, "there is another way up which I found quite by accident while exploring the tower some years ago as a possible bastion of defense."

"Another way!" Mark said, his eyes brightening. "Do the priests know of it?"

"No, lord. I never told anyone."

"And you'll take me?"

"Yes, lord."

Even as they spoke, Mandit Karr was leading them through the crowd. He told them about Bah-Ch'nanq, a mad old priest dedicated not to the god but to self-glory.

"The old man is insane, I think," Mandit Karr said. "And he's desperate, lord. He'll do whatever he has to."

"We've got to hurry," Mark said, as if the urgency of his words could lend wings to their feet. The crowd pushed and buffeted on all sides, but Mandit Karr had supplied Mark wisely with a cowl, which covered and hid his head and face. Finally they reached a point opposite the Tower of the God, two hundred yards across the square at the center of Purname City.

"I don't understand," Mark said. "How—"

"Underground, lord," said Mandit Karr. "Come."

They entered a building of sandstone, walked down a corridor, descended a flight of stairs. A sword-girted, saffron-robed priest stood at the bottom. As they approached he unsheathed the sword and stood facing them boldly. "This way is barred to all but the priesthood," he intoned.

"How did you find—" Mandit Karr blurted.

"Think you," laughed the young priest, "that you soldiers are the only ones with a desire to explore?"

For answer, Mandit Karr hurled himself at the priest. The sword lifted, flashed in the light of the single flambeaux that revealed a stone door behind the priest. Mandit Karr sagged heavily without a sound, the point of the blade protruding from the middle of his back.

Froth bubbled at his lips as he swung around impaled. "Go, lord!" he cried—and was dead.

While Otto Spade attacked the massive stone door, Mark rushed at the slayer-priest and struck him savagely in the face before the sword could be withdrawn from Mandit Karr's corpse. The priest slumped to the floor as Mark felt a sudden draft of air.

"The door!" Otto Spade cried. "Come on, Mark—"

Then Otto rushed back toward the foot of the stairs, got one foot against Mandit Karr's chest and tugged at the sword-hilt. The sword came loose with a terrible scraping sound and Otto Spade swung it once in a bright swift arc and the unconscious priest's head leaped from his shoulders. Mark turned away but Otto said:

"You didn't want a killer at your back, boy. Did you?"

"N-no," Mark said, fighting down sudden nausea, "you did what you had to."

Shoulder to shoulder, they went through the doorway. There was another flight of stairs, this one going up. It was carved in the living rock and seemed to rise endlessly, arcing tier on tier, toward the unseen sky. Mark climbed weaponless but Otto Spade carried the still-bloody sword with him, holding the hilt loosely in his big hand, the bloody tip scraping occasionally against the rock steps. The sound reminded Mark of the noise the sword had made being withdrawn from Mandit Karr's body.

He didn't feel like a god now.

He felt like anything but a god. He needed action to get his mind off the horror he had seen. He knew that—and grimly knew he was going to get it. But would he be in time?

IN THE TOWER room of the shrine Bah-Ch'nanq said: "Bring the girl to me."

One of the lesser priests dragged Susan across the room toward the fire. She struggled and tried to fight him off, but could not match his strength.

"Remove her garment," said the priest of Ch'nanq.

Susan fought furiously but felt her jumper torn from her. "You see," Bah-Ch'nanq said, "we don't have to hurt you yet. First we send down this garment, then another article of clothing, and another. When we finish with what you are wearing, if they haven't realized we are not going to be bested, we will start on your body."

Despite the firelight, Susan's face was very pale. "You're insane," she said. "You're absolutely insane."

Bah-Ch'nanq slapped her face without passion. Against the white of her skin a red welted handprint appeared. "Insane?" he repeated her word. "I think not. Desperate, devout—"

"Devout?" Susan screamed, wondering why she even bothered to stall for time, knowing no one could help her here. "You call yourself devout?"

Bah-Ch'nanq said something and one of the lesser priests went through the doorway with the girl's jumper. That left two lesser priests and Bah-Ch'nanq himself with Susan.

"We must not be driven from our world," the high priest said. "Last time we went like sheep—and what happened? Now they tell us we must go again."

"But your sun is going to explode. It isn't a question of heat. It won't burn this world. It will vaporize it!"

"If the god-sun is angry," began Bah-Ch'nanq, "and if we offer him a sacrifice your—"

He got no further. Behind the fire, something stirred. Rock grated on rock. One of the lesser priests unsheathed his sword and rushed around the fire. There was the clang of metal on metal. Sparks flew.

"Mark!" Susan cried in disbelief.

UNARMED, Mark ran toward them as the second priest drew his sword. Mark crouched, drew a brand from the fire, hurled it full in the priest's face and saw him scream and fall back. He heard a hoarse shout behind him and did not know if Otto Spade or his Purnamese antagonist had been impaled.

"Mark! Look out, he's got a knife!"

The knife gleamed in Bah-Ch'nanq's hand, red with the light of the fire. He crouched before Mark, holding the knife below his waist loosely, expertly, ready to slash upward with it. Mark wished he had held the brand.

"You!" the high priest bellowed hysterically. "False god! You're responsible! You—"

And he rushed at Mark, slashing upward with the knife.

Mark felt the blade sear against his ribs and felt the warm surge of blood down his flank. Then he was grappling with the old man, who possessed wild, incredible strength.

They fought back and forth before the fire, Mark intent on the wrist of the hand that held the knife, trying to keep it away from his body, Bah-Ch'nanq belabored Mark's face with his free hand, punching, clawing, ripping for the eyes with stiff fingers.

Mark stumbled and fell, feeling the old priest's bony strength come down on top of him, feeling the bite of the knife blade against his throat. They lay there for a moment, unmoving, the knife digging a little valley in the muscle wall of Mark's throat but not piercing the skin, both Mark's hands on the arm that wielded the blade...

Then Bah-Ch'nanq's legs began to drum, the knees digging painfully into Mark's abdomen and groin. The knife pressed deeper, puncturing skin. There was a roaring in Mark's ears and a picture flashed before his eyes as time seemed suspended of the triumphant high priest parading before his people the corpse of the false god. If that happened, two hundred million Purnamese would perish because they would not obey the Operation Disaster evacuation orders, the Earthmen would also be slaughtered, and Anson Channing's name would never be honored…

Mad eyes hovered inches over Mark's. Spittle dribbled down on his face as, millimeter by millimeter, the knife bit deeper. Mark kicked out with his legs and for a moment the knife was withdrawn as Bah-Ch'nanq screamed in pain and surprise. Mark used the single moment he had to grasp the light but powerful body with both his hands and heave as he simultaneously kicked up again with his legs.

Screaming, Bah-Ch'nanq plunged into the fire.

He rolled over, still screaming, and got to his knees in the flames. He crawled and lifted one hand, still holding the knife. Then the flames enveloped him and he seemed to shrivel in their fiery embrace.

All at once there was a charnel smell in the room. Susan came to Mark as he stood up, and swooned against him. Mark held her, supporting her weight on his arm, and looked beyond the fire. One of the lesser priests was dead. The other, his hand in the air over his head and a look of fear on his face, had been disarmed. Panting and bleeding from a cut on the cheek, Otto Spade watched him warily.

"Let's go down there," Mark said.

"They'll accept you now, boy," Otto Spade predicted. "As their god."

"If it will help, then let them."

Otto Spade nodded. "Then let them," he repeated the words. "If only Hurley Jamison had let them do that twenty years ago, all this wouldn't have happened. They'll do anything you say, boy. Anything at all. They'll evacuate this world."

"They'd better," Mark said. "And fast."

Trailing behind their prisoner, who would tell how the god's magic had been stronger than the high priest's, and leading a dazed Susan Jamison, Mark and Otto Spade went downstairs and outside to the waiting throngs of Purnamese.

Otto Spade was right.

They worshipped Mark Channing as a god.

CHAPTER TEN

THE EXPLOSION was awesome.

It was not meant for human eyes. It could not be understood by human intellect. It was a sun going up in a millisecond in a blaze of energy that equaled all the energy given forth in that same millisecond by all the stars of the galaxy.

Supernova!

Mark stood with Otto Spade, Captain MacCready, Dr. Culcross and Susan Jamison on the observation deck of the Operation Disaster ship, watching it. Several weeks had passed—weeks in which, following their god, the Purnamese had obediently embarked in the fleet of rescue ships, which had been waiting for them since the last evacuation. Technicians were even now administering suspended animation, so that a race of people could be preserved until a new home somewhere in the depths of space was found for them.

"How can you ever forgive us?" Susan asked Mark. "All of us. We've been so cruel."

"Cruel, hell," said Captain MacCready. "Thanks to my bullheadedness, we had a mutiny on our hands."

Otto Spade smiled. "But it didn't last when they saw that mob of Purnamese coming down on the ship, with me and Mark at their head."

Dr. Culcross nodded. "There were fatalities, though. Men died…"

"What gets me," Otto Spade said, "is how they'll go unpunished. The ones who did it, I mean. A man can't spend two life sentences in prison."

"These men won't even get to spend one," MacCready said. "I never had a chance to tell you. When the counter-mutiny broke out, the original mutineers were torn to pieces."

For a while they stood in silence, watching the incandescent death of a star. Already all the Purnamese planets had been vaporized. Already the vast cloud of gas which had been a sun was speeding out into space at near-light speed and would, in another few hundred years, form a nebula.

"There seems to be a likely planet circling the star Fok-Dennier 14," Dr. Culcross said. "We're going out there to investigate. It ought to make a new home for these poor people, and give them a chance to find civilization again."

Death, Mark thought, and life in its wake. The human cycle.

"What will we call the new world?" Susan asked.

"Why, Purname, of course," Mark said, and took her hand.

THE END

If you've enjoyed this book, you will not want to miss these terrific titles...

ARMCHAIR SCI-FI & HORROR DOUBLE NOVELS, $12.95 each

D-11   **PERIL OF THE STARMEN** by Kris Neville
THE STRANGE INVASION by Murray Leinster

D-12   **THE STAR LORD** by Boyd Ellanby
CAPTIVES OF THE FLAME by Samuel R. Delaney

D-13   **MEN OF THE MORNING STAR** by Edmund Hamilton
PLANET FOR PLUNDER by Hal Clement and Sam Merwin, Jr.

D-14   **ICE CITY OF THE GORGON** by Chester S. Geier and Richard Shaver
WHEN THE WORLD TOTTERED by Lester Del Rey

D-15   **WORLDS WITHOUT END** by Clifford D. Simak
THE LAVENDER VINE OF DEATH by Don Wilcox

D-16   **SHADOW ON THE MOON** by Joe Gibson
ARMAGEDDON EARTH by Geoff St. Reynard

D-17   **THE GIRL WHO LOVED DEATH** by Paul W. Fairman
SLAVE PLANET by Laurence M. Janifer

D-18   **SECOND CHANCE** by J. F. Bone
MISSION TO A DISTANT STAR by Frank Belknap Long

D-19   **THE SYNDIC** by C. M. Kornbluth
FLIGHT TO FOREVER by Poul Anderson

D-20   **SOMEWHERE I'LL FIND YOU** by Milton Lesser
THE TIME ARMADA by Fox B. Holden

ARMCHAIR SCIENCE FICTION CLASSICS, $12.95 each

C-4   **CORPUS EARTHLING**
by Louis Charbonneau

C-5   **THE TIME DISSOLVER**
by Jerry Sohl

C-6   **WEST OF THE SUN**
by Edgar Pangborn

ARMCHAIR SCIENCE FICTION & HORROR GEMS SERIES, $12.95 each

G-1   **SCIENCE FICTION GEMS, Vol. One**
Isaac Asimov and others

G-2   **HORROR GEMS, Vol. One**
Carl Jacobi and others

If you've enjoyed this book, you will not want to miss these terrific titles…

ARMCHAIR SCI-FI, FANTASY, & HORROR DOUBLE NOVELS, $12.95 each

D-21   **EMPIRE OF EVIL** by Robert Arnette
      THE SIGN OF THE TIGER by Alan E. Nourse & J. A. Meyer

D-22   **OPERATION SQUARE PEG** by Frank Belknap Long
      ENCHANTRESS OF VENUS by Leigh Brackett

D-23   **THE LIFE WATCH** by Lester Del Rey
      CREATURES OF THE ABYSS by Murray Leinster

D-24   **LEGION OF LAZARUS** by Edmond Hamilton
      STAR HUNTER by Andre Norton

D-25   **EMPIRE OF WOMEN** by John Fletcher
      ONE OF OUR CITIES IS MISSING by Irving Cox

D-26   **THE WRONG SIDE OF PARADISE** by Raymond F. Jones
      THE INVOLUNTARY IMMORTALS by Rog Phillips

D-27   **EARTH QUARTER** by Damon Knight
      ENVOY TO NEW WORLDS by Keith Laumer

D-28   **SLAVES TO THE METAL HORDE** by Milton Lesser
      HUNTERS OUT OF TIME by Joseph E. Kelleam

D-29   **RX JUPITER SAVE US** by Ward Moore
      BEWARE THE USURPERS by Geoff St. Reynard

D-30   **SECRET OF THE SERPENT** by Don Wilcox
      CRUSADE ACROSS THE VOID by Dwight V. Swain

ARMCHAIR SCIENCE FICTION CLASSICS, $12.95 each

C-7   **THE SHAVER MYSTERY, Book One**
     by Richard S. Shaver

C-8   **THE SHAVER MYSTERY, Book Two**
     by Richard S. Shaver

C-9   **MURDER IN SPACE** by David V. Reed
     by David V. Reed

ARMCHAIR MASTERS OF SCIENCE FICTION SERIES, $16.95 each

M-3   **MASTERS OF SCIENCE FICTION, Vol. Three**
     Robert Sheckley, "The Perfect Woman" and other tales

M-4   **MASTERS OF SCIENCE FICTION, Vol. Four**
     Mack Reynolds, "Stowaway" and other tales

If you've enjoyed this book, you will not want to miss these terrific titles…

ARMCHAIR SCI-FI & HORROR DOUBLE NOVELS, $12.95 each

D-31   **A HOAX IN TIME** by Keith Laumer
         INSIDE EARTH by Poul Anderson

D-32   **TERROR STATION** by Dwight V. Swain
         THE WEAPON FROM ETERNITY by Dwight V. Swain

D-33   **THE SHIP FROM INFINITY** by Edmond Hamilton
         TAKEOFF by C. M. Kornbluth

D-34   **THE METAL DOOM** by David H. Keller
         TWELVE TIMES ZERO by Howard Browne

D-35   **HUNTERS OUT OF SPACE** by Joseph Kelleam
         INVASION FROM THE DEEP by Paul W. Fairman,

D-36   **THE BEES OF DEATH** by Robert Moore Williams
         A PLAGUE OF PYTHONS by Frederick Pohl

D-37   **THE LORDS OF QUARMALL** by Fritz Leiber and Harry Fischer
         BEACON TO ELSEWHERE by James H. Schmitz

D-38   **BEYOND PLUTO** by John S. Campbell
         ARTERY OF FIRE by Thomas N. Scortia

D-39   **SPECIAL DELIVERY** by Kris Neville
         NO TIME FOR TOFFEE by Charles F. Meyers

D-40   **RECALLED TO LIFE** by Robert Silverberg
         JUNGLE IN THE SKY by Milton Lesser

ARMCHAIR SCIENCE FICTION CLASSICS, $12.95 each

C-10   **MARS IS MY DESTINATION**
         by Frank Belknap Long

C-11   **SPACE PLAGUE**
         by George O. Smith

C-12   **SO SHALL YE REAP**
         by Rog Phillips

ARMCHAIR SCIENCE FICTION & HORROR GEMS SERIES, $12.95 each

G-3   **SCIENCE FICTION GEMS, Vol. Two**
        James Blish and others

G-4   **HORROR GEMS, Vol. Two**
        Joseph Payne Brennan and others

If you've enjoyed this book, you will not want to miss these terrific titles…

ARMCHAIR SCI-FI, FANTASY, & HORROR DOUBLE NOVELS, $12.95 each

D-41   **FULL CYCLE** by Clifford D. Simak
IT WAS THE DAY OF THE ROBOT by Frank Belknap Long

D-42   **THIS CROWDED EARTH** by Robert Bloch
REIGN OF THE TELEPUPPETS by Daniel Galouye

D-43   **THE CRISPIN AFFAIR** by Jack Sharkey
THE RED HELL OF JUPITER by Paul Ernst

D-44   **PLANET OF DREAD** by Dwight V. Swain
WE THE MACHINE by Gerald Vance

D-45   **THE STAR HUNTER** by Edmond Hamilton
THE ALIEN by Raymond F. Jones

D-46   **WORLD OF IF** by Rog Phillips
SLAVE RAIDERS FROM MERCURY by Don Wilcox

D-47   **THE ULTIMATE PERIL** by Robert Abernathy
PLANET OF SHAME by Bruce Elliot

D-48   **THE FLYING EYES** by J. Hunter Holly
SOME FABULOUS YONDER by Phillip Jose Farmer

D-49   **THE COSMIC BUNGLARS** by Geoff St. Reynard
THE BUTTONED SKY by Geoff St. Reynard

D-50   **TYRANTS OF TIME** by Milton Lesser
PARIAH PLANET by Murray Leinster

ARMCHAIR SCIENCE FICTION CLASSICS, $12.95 each

C-13   **SUNKEN WORLD**
by Stanton A. Coblentz

C-14   **THE LAST VIAL**
by Sam McClatchie, M. D.

C-15   **WE WHO SURVIVED (THE FIFTH ICE AGE)**
by Sterling Noel

ARMCHAIR MASTERS OF SCIENCE FICTION SERIES, $16.95 each

MS-5   **MASTERS OF SCIENCE FICTION, Vol. Five**
Winston K. Marks—Test Colony and other tales

MS-6   **MASTERS OF SCIENCE FICTION, Vol. Six**
Fritz Leiber—Deadly Moon and other tales

If you've enjoyed this book, you will not want to miss these terrific titles…

ARMCHAIR SCI-FI & HORROR DOUBLE NOVELS, $12.95 each

D-51   **A GOD NAMED SMITH** by Henry Slesar
           WORLDS OF THE IMPERIUM by Keith Laumer

D-52   **CRAIG'S BOOK** by Don Wilcox
           EDGE OF THE KNIFE by H. Beam Piper

D-53   **THE SHINING CITY** by Rena M. Vale
           THE RED PLANET by Russ Winterbotham

D-54   **THE MAN WHO LIVED TWICE** by Rog Phillips
           VALLEY OF THE CROEN by Lee Tarbell

D-55   **OPERATION DISASTER** by Milton Lesser
           LAND OF THE DAMNED by Berkeley Livingston

D-56   **CAPTIVE OF THE CENTAURIANESS** by Poul Anderson
           A PRINCESS OF MARS by Edgar Rice Burroughs

D-57   **THE NON-STATISTICAL MAN** by Raymond F. Jones
           MISSION FROM MARS by Rick Conroy

D-58   **INTRUDERS FROM THE STARS** by Ross Rocklynne
           FLIGHT OF THE STARLING by Chester S. Geier

D-59   **COSMIC SABOTEUR** by Frank M. Robinson
           LOOK TO THE STARS by Willard Hawkins

D-60   **THE MOON IS HELL!** by John W. Campbell, Jr.
           THE GREEN WORLD by Hal Clement

ARMCHAIR SCIENCE FICTION CLASSICS, $12.95 each

C-16   **THE SHAVER MYSTERY, Book Three**
           by Richard S. Shaver

C-17   **THE GIRLS FROM PLANET 5**
           by Richard Wilson

C-18   **THE FOURTH "R"**
           by George O. Smith

ARMCHAIR SCIENCE FICTION & HORROR GEMS SERIES, $12.95 each

G-5   **SCIENCE FICTION GEMS, Vol. Three**
           C. M. Kornbluth and others

G-6   **HORROR GEMS, Vol. Three**
           August Derleth and others

MASS MURDER SWEEPS THE U. S.

It all had happened so quickly. One moment everything was tranquil, the next moment the entire populace of the United States was trying to kill itself. But what was the cause? Two scientists who were lucky enough to have survived the carnage, along with a traitorous alien from the depths of outer space, knew the grim truth—the world had been invaded by a conquering horde from a distant planet.

But the invading extraterrestrial force, in spite of its awesome power, was still vulnerable to human reprisal unless it was able to recover a fantastic ancient weapon buried deep in the Bad Lands of Utah—a weapon that would forever leave humanity in subjugation. Could the alien forces be stopped in time? It was a mad race against time, with mankind's fate hanging in the balance.

CAST OF CHARACTERS

DALE NORTON
He was out for a stroll one night when he suddenly changed into a psychopathic killer—like everyone else in America.

JARVIS WITSON
This aging scientist escaped the carnage of the first night of the invasion, but becoming an alien prisoner wasn't much better.

JETTO
Not your typical dictator with dreams of ultimate power—he didn't care if his conquered minions were all dead!

NUMBER 1
He held the secret to the complete alien takeover of Earth—and it got him branded a traitor and thrown into prison!

FU-TA
He was the number two man in the massive invasion of Earth, but how loyal was he to the brutal plans of conquest?

GENERAL SANDERS
Being the top military man in humanity's counterattack didn't mean he was necessarily in command.

LAND OF
THE
DAMNED

By
BERKELEY LIVINGSTON

ARMCHAIR FICTION
PO Box 4369, Medford, Oregon 97504

CHAPTER ONE

AUGUST 21, 1970!

Dale Norton would not, *could not,* forget that date. It was engraved on his brain in letters of flame.

The tasseled corn hung heavy. The dry grass rustled softly under his feet. There was the familiar, yet always strange odor of rich earth and that which came from the earth: the corn and wheat and all the ripe fruition of Nature's boundless goodness. And Dale Norton was glad to be alive and part of it all.

Blaze, Dale's dog and boon companion moved on silent, padded feet beside him, turning his shaggy head now and then in worshipful glance at his master. The sky was heavy with stars. Dale had never seen a more beautiful night. He saw through the corner of his eye a falling pinpoint of light explode in momentary brilliance, then die.

"Guess summer's about over, pooch," he said softly. "Look!" He pointed to the heavens. Blaze's tail wagged furiously and he bounded back and forth, as though he thought his master had given him a command to play. But Norton's eyes were riveted on the heavens. The Perseids, those meteorites whose visit to our atmosphere were an unfailing August occurrence, were out in force. Norton could not remember when he had seen so many of them.

Yet on this night there was something strange about them. For a moment he could not think what it was. Then it came to him. They were not all meteors! For some of them did not explode in flaming incandescence. These passed overhead with a speed beyond human comprehension. He could not take his eyes from the spectacular display. More and more of the strange phenomena passed above him.

Norton didn't remember at what precise moment panic took him in its grip. The transition between peace and fear was an instant of which he had no cognizance. He only knew that his clothes had become too tight. That his throat had become parched. He tore his clothes from his body with frantic fingers, ripping away buttons and tearing at the restraining cloth until he was completely nude!

He panted and gasped as if each breath he took was his last. A sudden sound made him whirl about. Blaze had appeared from between a stand of corn and was regarding him with cocked ear. The dog whined in fear. And Norton echoed the sound—only in the man's voice there was something horrible beyond words. Blaze's head sunk down and the hackles rose along his furry back. Slowly, he began to retreat.

Norton crouched low. His mouth opened and sounds—they could not be words, there was nothing human in them—reached out to stop the dog. It stopped. The man advanced in a slow shambling trot toward it. The dog's head lifted in a sort of puzzled movement, as if it were not quite certain of itself.

Then, before it could move, Norton leaped on it!

Blaze whirled even as a grasping hand slid along the fur. Almost it was clear of the clutching fingers, but then they found a grip on a hind leg. And Blaze howled once in pain and fear. For the man had twisted savagely at the leg until there was a sound as of breaking wood.

The dog's head swept downward and sideways in a swift movement that was sheer reflex. Its teeth slashed at the naked, hairy forearm lying on its flank. Blood streamed in a crimson tide where the teeth ripped into the flesh. Then the man's hands came up to meet in a vise around the furry throat of the dog. There was an instant of whirling movement when the man and dog were as one. Then Norton flung the dog to the ground. His foot came down in a terrible, stomping crash on the small of the dog's back at its hindquarters. His right arm pulled the dog's head back—and Dale Norton sank his teeth in the dog's throat and ripped savagely until the flesh tore and his mouth became filled with the hot salty blood!

THE man, it was no longer a man, but rather some strange sort of brute being, lifted his head from the grotesque body of the dog. The head swayed back and forth in odd movement that was like a person in sorrow. The head stopped its shaking. The man arose until it stood almost erect, but not quite, as though the crouch it was in was as far as it could get to the perpendicular. Turning, it began an ape-like shambling toward the small cluster of buildings at the far edge of the first orderly row of corn. Blood stained the face into a red mask out of which his eyes gleamed in warm, animal pleasure.

He didn't seem to notice the gravel of the path. If he did, he paid no attention to the fact that the coarse bits of rock tore at the tender flesh of his soles. The path wound past the steel-ribbed fence of the big pen. Grunting animal sounds took his attention. He paused for an instant, then moved across the grass to investigate. The fence gleamed in an oddly broken pattern in the moonlight, as if it were stained on some parts of its usual gleaming surface.

He stumbled over an obstruction. Stopping, he bent to see what it was. It proved to be a short, double-bitted axe, imbedded in a cord of wood. He pulled it free and continued his advance to the pen. His nostrils dilated and his mouth loosened in a grin as he smelled the familiar odor, sweet and warm, of blood. He became aware too, of a strange chomping sound. Then there was silence. He peered down from over the top rail of the fence. The coarse grin broadened and a trickle of saliva made its way down the cleft chin. A chuckling sound, half of pleasure and half of anticipation came from his throat. His fingers fumbled at the latch, then it opened wide and he stepped within.

The brood sow regarded him with a quiet look. Scattered around the pen were the mutilated figures of a half dozen piglets. On the ground, below the ugly snout was the body of another, its belly ripped open by her tusks. Her snout dripped blood. The man looked only once at the dead animals. His interest was only in the living. For they too had to die!

For in that delicate instrument of flesh and bone which only a short time before had been that which made him different from the animal world, had only a single thought. To kill! To kill whatever living thing came into its path!

The two moved simultaneously in each other's direction. Nor did either give warning. But the man was much faster. The blade of the axe described a flashing half-circle of light before it found haven in the sow's skull. The man looked down at the body and once more there was the sound of mad laughter. Then, without another look at either the animal or the axe, he turned and walked from the pen.

NEITHER beast nor man nor machine moved on the broad, four-lane highway. Only the shambling figure of Dale Norton moved on the concrete. The moon beat down in pale indifference to the eerie scene. Nor was it any more indifferent than the man. He passed an overturned car. He peered into its interior with an incurious glance. The driver, his head bent at an impossible angle was lying half in the seat and half on the floor. He was dead. Norton moved around the front of the car to the other side. Two people, a man and a woman, were locked in an embrace on the ground. They too were dead. But theirs was a death more horrible than the driver's. For his had been one of accident.

The two on the ground had fought each other to the death. Neither had any clothes on. The woman had a broken neck. Clenched in her teeth was the man's ear. She had bitten it off in her death struggle. Her fingers were around his throat as were his around hers. Norton nudged the bodies with his toe. They moved stiffly, then rolled back into the same position of frozen immobility. He went back on the highway.

A dozen times he came across similar scenes. Always, they were dead. And always they had found it necessary to remove their clothes. The positions were different. That was all.

He walked along, the only living thing to be seen on the whole plane of that land. A human robot, moving in patternless, purposeless motion. The moon sank below the horizon. And still the figure of Dale Norton strode on. A grey murk rose up out of the east. Mist came from the edge of the meadow, flanking the broad highway. The grayness lighted into a pale effulgence of rosy color. The rim of the sun appeared from the edge of the earth. Higher and higher it rose until its rays struck full into his eyes. And a terrible transformation took place in the man.

His mouth opened and bestial, inhuman, tortured sounds came from the twisted, grimacing lips. His hands lifted and tore at his head with clawing fingers, tore until the black hair that covered his scalp did so only in patches. A last, horror-filled shriek rasped from his throat. And he fell to the ground. His body twitched in epileptic-like paroxysms, then was stilled.

DALE NORTON turned and rolled to his side. He groaned with the effort it took. Every muscle in his body ached as though he had been beaten. He arose and looked down at his naked body. Shame swept over him at the sight. It was a shame born out of nothingness, for he was incapable of thought. As it had come, so did it leave him, instantly, nor did he wonder at the feeling.

The sun was overhead. And he felt hunger. He moved his head from side to side, his eyes peering keenly into the underbrush for sight of anything that moved. He grunted in disappointment for he saw that nothing disturbed the rank grass. He rubbed a hand across a stubbled cheek. The hair rasped strongly. It puzzled him, for instinct still played a role in his life and he never permitted the hair to grow for more than a day. That, too, like his feeling of shame passed quickly.

He stepped back on the highway. Something told him to move in the direction of the sun's rising. Time after time, he passed the rusted wrecks of machines strange to his eyes. Their once sleek bodies, chromium-plated, were now rusted and misshapen. He gave them no more than a cursory glance.

The sun sank below the horizon. The moon rose. And now he came to the reaches of a large city. There was no light illuminating the small homes of the suburb through which he passed. Nor was there any human being to be seen on the wide, paved streets. It was a town dead for all practical purposes. He did not think it strange that such a thing could be.

He passed a trolley which, like the homes he had seen, was without light. It stood motionless upon the street. A voice, hoarse, emotionless, yet which held implications of terror, suddenly called to him:

"Hist!"

He paused.

Once again the voice called:

"Hey there!"

He turned and peered at the trolley. Then he saw it. First he saw the head. Then he saw the rest of the body within the streetcar. An arm came through the broken glass of one of the windows and motioned him forward. He came forward on wary, tiptoeing feet.

Norton peered up at the face at the window. It was a thin, emaciated face. Hunger and terror had given it lines nature had not intended it to have. A wispy beard covered the face from the cheekbones to the chin.

"Quick, friend," the voice said. "In here! Before the guard makes its rounds."

The words meant nothing to Norton. Guards? Rounds? From around the corner of a bisecting street there came the sounds of marching feet. Once again the voice urged, "quickly!" This time Norton didn't hesitate. Before the vanguard of the watch came around the corner, he was through one of the open windows and crouching on the floor beside the stranger. His body bulked large against the tiny one of the man within the car. Words came from the little man, as he peered from the window, nor did he turn to look at Norton once he was in the safety of the trolley.

"Are you mad, that you walk about naked in the hours between dark and dawn? Life means little these days, true enough. But at least you are free. If one of them catches you…"

He ducked his head down suddenly, in the midst of warnings, and came face to face with Norton, for the first time. The moon, slanting down through the windows shone full upon his face.

The bearded face stared at him as if he was seeing a ghost.

"You! You!" the voice rasped hoarsely. "Dale! Dale Norton! Oh no! Not to you!"

NORTON, hunkered down on his heels, gave the other a glance of bewilderment. The other went on in a low voice, as if to himself:

"And why not Dale Norton? Is he so different from the rest? Only mentally. And first—" he left off and peered closely into the other's countenance. There was fear in the old man's eyes, then. After a moment he sighed deeply. "No. No, the kill mood is gone. If I only knew how long…" again there was the reflective stop. "H'm. His beard is long," he resumed in his monologue. "But that can mean little. And it can mean a lot. If only I could break through to his…" he stopped again, this time to listen. For Norton had broken his silence. From the other's sub-conscious, a small wave had broken through:

"Beard—too—long. Shave everyday. Norton. Norton. I'm Norton."

Excitement sent the little man's voice into a squeak:

"You're coming through, man. Think hard! Who are you?"

Silence.

Then the monotone. "Norton. I'm Norton. I'm *Norton!*" The last had been a hoarse acknowledgment of a fact that was understood. The spell he was in was broken. And with the return of Norton's mental faculties, there came recognition of the little man.

"Witson!" Norton exclaimed. "Jarvis Witson. What are..." he became aware then, of his condition. "Holy cats! Someone took my clothes!" he muttered.

"Shh!" Witson hissed sharply. He had been on the alert ever since he had first heard the approach of the patrol. Norton heard the sound of pounding feet also. A voice, hoarse, strident, shouted:

"Rota! The trolley! Numbers, 3, 7, 4, 8, follow me."

"Quick..." Witson called a low warning. "Down...as low as you can."

Norton hunkered down on his haunches as far as he was able. There was an urgency in Witson's voice that didn't permit questioning, then. Booted feet sounded in rising crescendo. They came up the steps of the trolley. The two men, crouched behind the bulwark of the seat heard the guard come to a halt as he stepped within the motorman's cab. Then a narrow beam of light came to life and swept down the narrow aisle.

The darkness was intense when the beam snapped off. And then the guard, satisfied that no one was hiding in the trolley, trotted down the stairs.

Witson's eyes gleamed in satisfaction. They had outwitted the guard. And Norton's calf muscles cramped into a tight knot. He shifted his weight, leaning against the seat as he did so, it gave suddenly, rolling back on squeaking rollers. The squealing sound was as the knell of doom. For the guard came to a halt. And his voice rose in warning, as he ran back to the trolley:

"Guards! Mio! This way!"

"Run for it!" Witson commanded.

In an instant he was out the window, Norton close behind him. They sped across the street. While behind them, the guards came swiftly around the sides of the trolley. A half dozen fingers of light moved to pick them up. One struck the figures and whining, whiplash-sounds screamed toward them. Norton sped past a tree and something struck it as, his body was shielded, momentarily by its trunk. There was a burst of flame, an explosive crack, and the tree slowly toppled to the ground. Fear lent wings to the feet of the two refugees.

They ran down a passageway between two homes. The concrete of the path continued to a gate, set in a stone wall. The gate was open. Norton in the lead, came to an abrupt halt. It was an impasse. Before them was a screen fence. And beyond it he saw the moonlight reflecting on water. There was no place for them to go. To either side was open ground. Already, he heard the running sound of the guards. Without an instant's hesitation, he ran to the fence and scaled it, hanging by his fingers for a second, gauging the distance to the water. He dropped, there was not the smallest splash when he struck. Witson followed immediately. He was not as good a diver as Norton. There was more than a perceptible splash when he lit.

NORTON swam at an angle for the far bank. Behind him, a few feet, he heard Witson. Once again the lights came into play. And suddenly the water boiled in a puff of smoke, just past his head.

"Swim under water," he called to Witson. "That tree upstream—safe under it."

Norton scrambled up the bank, turned and dragged Witson after him. The little man was visibly tired. But there was no time to rest. Norton recognized their haven. It was a forest preserve. He remembered the river they had swum, also. It meandered in zigzag fashion through the preserve for its entire length. And somewhere, nearby he hoped, there should be a narrow, wooden span, which crossed it.

"Wait here," he whispered.

Without a further word, he went flat on his belly and squirmed forward until he lay on the edge of the bank, only a little ways past the tree. The marsh grass hid him well. Lifting his head, he peered up and down the river's length. A grin appeared on his face. The bridge lay a hundred yards upstream.

He crawled back to Witson.

"Follow me," he said. And set off at a trot. Witson panted after him. They ran for perhaps three minutes. The older man noticed that they were on a well-defined path. The path led past a small, railed enclosure. Wire cages were set behind the bars. Witson could not see whether there was anything alive in the cages. There was no sound from them. The path led in a circle around the small animal zoo. At the far end was a house or rather a log cabin. Norton made straight for it.

There were two dead people in it, a man and a woman.

Norton's face was twisted in grief as he knelt at their side. They lay in a close embrace, as though death had caught them in the midst of a kiss. Neither had a stitch of clothes on. And Norton's horror-stricken eyes saw that it was not love which held them so close, but hate. For they had died, tearing at each other's throats—with their teeth. The man's lips were glued to the woman's throat at the point where the jugular vein had once pulsed in living. Her face had only rested against his. So it seemed to Norton, until he looked closer. Then he saw that she had already accomplished her purpose. The man's throat had been ripped wide open.

Norton straightened and staggered over to the doorway and was violently sick for a moment. He felt a hand on his shoulder and a gentle voice ask:

"Friends?"

"Ye—yes. The Antolinis." he mumbled. Then louder, "what horrible thing has happened? I—I seem to remember other—horrors like these."

Witson pulled him back into the cabin. He made Norton sit while he roamed the narrow confines of the small cabin. There wasn't much to be seen. Simply furnished, it held little of luxury, except a fine radio set. Witson sighed audibly as he went to the set and fiddled with the dials. He did it hap-hazardly, as if he was only wasting time until Norton, sitting at an inside table, would regain his composure. Witson was startled as the radio light glowed bright, then faded but did not go out. Almost feverishly, Witson manipulated the dials. A humming sound was heard.

The man at the table lifted his head from his arms and looked dazedly about him when the sound of a strange human voice came into the oppressive air of the cabin.

The voice said:

"B. B. C. calling New York. B. B. C. calling New York…" There was a second's silence, then the voice came on again, "Come in New York." Another pause, then the announcer's voice once again, this time it held overtones of fright, "what is wrong over there? Why don't you answer? What is…?"

Witson snapped the set off with a muttered imprecation, "damn them! Our last hope—gone!"

The man at the table shook his head. When he spoke there was a brittle quality to his voice that was obviously foreign to it for Witson jerked around at the sound and looked keenly into Norton's face as if he feared that the other's mind had given way under the blows it had taken. But a single glance at the squared jaw and narrowed eyes told him otherwise.

Norton said:

"What is the date?"

Witson looked surprise.

"Date?" he asked hesitantly. "Why—why, I think it's the fifth—yes, the fifth of September."

CHAPTER TWO

NORTON'S eyes widened. Two weeks had passed, two weeks that were taken from him and of which he had no memory. He looked at the bodies of his friends and turned quickly away. Perhaps he was better off that it was so? He came right to the point, then:

"What happened on August twenty-first?"

Witson closed his eyes and recited in voice, slow and heavy with hidden passion, the events that had come to pass since that day:

"The United States was invaded by a people from outer space. Yes, from a universe far beyond the confines of any we know. And in a single day they accomplished that which we thought would be the impossible. They conquered us!"

"No!" Norton burst out.

Witson thrust out a frail, blue-veined hand to halt the other's pent up words.

"Yes!" he continued. "They did. With machines and weapons beyond any of our devising. First, and I must confess that how is a mystery to me, they spread through these machines an over-powering compunction to every human mind within their reach the desire to kill. I don't know how many millions were killed in the first night. I am afraid to guess.

"They came in immense space ships. Hundreds of ships containing thousands of men in each ship. That night, every radio set in the country went out. Every means of communication went dead. We were completely isolated from the rest of the world. And that reminds me. The radio in this cabin was on. I wonder…" He moved to the wall and snapped at the light switch. Nothing happened. "Hmmm. Now that's odd," he said in a low tone. "Radio goes on, yet there's no light."

A ghost-smile flickered on Norton's lips. He remembered that little oddity of Witson's. The ruminative, whispered speculations he held with himself. It somehow brought an air of reality to the whole fantastic and terrible situation. Norton explained the phenomena:

"Nothing very mysterious in that, Jarvis. The set doesn't need any electrical current to operate."

Witson's right eyebrow raised. It gave him an odd pensive look. "And how do you know that, my friend?" he asked.

"I built that set. A couple of months back," Norton replied.

"I see. Another one of your experiments, I presume?"

"Right. Electronics. But too complicated to explain. At least right now. The important thing, to get back to it, is what do we do now?"

Witson looked oddly pleased.

"Right to the point, eh Norton? I've always admired you for that faculty, as you remember. It was the reason why I told you to go in for research, when you were taking my course in anthropology. The dust of the ages was not meant for you. Yet the dust has come to settle on the present."

"Elaborate."

Witson looked to the outside before he went on. The familiar pattern of a new day's birth was beginning to unfold. He brought his glance back to Norton.

"Those space ships bore the symbol of the four forces! Mu and Lemuria! Perhaps Atlantis also. Those fabled lands *did* exist!"

Suddenly Norton had a vivid memory of a bygone day. A half dozen undergraduates lounging about the bachelor apartment of Jarvis Witson, head of the Archeology department of the university. And Witson expounding his theories. He even remembered some of the conversation, *"There are as many reasons to believe that the civilizations of Mu and Atlantis did not perish, as there are to the affirmative,"* Witson had said. *"After all, it is all in the approach. I like to think that I am open minded. Research has brought many things to light about these lands. And scientists have not answered any of the questions involved. Instead, many of them, in particular those whose names are considered the great, passed off the discoveries as either not genuine or too minute in themselves to present a worthwhile problem for investigation."*

THERE had been some further talk about books, and about references that could be found to substantiate Witson's theory, even in the Bible. Then it had broken up.

"Still riding that horse, Witson?" Norton asked.

Anger flamed in the frail man's eyes. Words blazed from his lips:

"I know! I heard them talk of it. The one they call, Jetto. I even know why they are here."

Norton's chin dropped. Then his eyes narrowed. Had Witson lost his senses? No! The old man was angry, yes, but a sane anger, directed at the disbelief shown his words.

"Sorry," Norton apologized. He became aware that day was breaking. And the problem of what they were going to do was still unanswered.

"Look," he said. "The sun'll be up in a few minutes. And I imagine that the patrol, which chased us, has reported that we are somewhere in the vicinity. We'll be sitting ducks here. Do you know of any place where we will be safe, for a while?"

Witson nodded that he did. But when Norton started for the door, he stopped him.

"Can't go out like that," he said. "Got to get some clothes—hmmm. Should be some here."

Norton gulped. Fred Antolini and his wife had been very dear friends of his. The thought of wearing some of the dead man's apparel gave him a sick feeling. Swinging about, Norton made for the clothes closet and after rummaging around came out with a pair of slacks and a heavy, flannel shirt. They fit him fairly well. He was even luckier with the shoes and socks. They fit perfectly.

Witson stopped on the threshold. He turned to Norton and said, apologetically:

"I—I hope you know how to get out of this?"

"You mean the forest preserve?"

"Yes. Once I have oriented myself, then—"

Norton laughed heartily. It did him good. Somehow the laugh helped to dispel some of the gloom.

"Just tell me where you want to go," he suggested. "I'll get us there."

"Well, you know that little college near the village of Rook Park? I've been hiding out in the basement of the school."

NORTON took the lead. He struck straight for the forested center of the park. Fifteen minutes of walking and they had reached the outskirts of the preserve. Norton proceeded with a greater caution, then. The trees were cut off sharply at the edge of one of the streets. He did not want to come into the open before he made sure that there was no one around. They lay on the ground behind the protecting foliage of a large bush. The street was deserted.

He peered between the close-pressed branches and saw the pointed spire of the school chapel. It wasn't far off. But there was the whole of a city block to traverse before they reached it. Once more he surveyed the situation. There was little choice. They were at the farthest edge of the preserve. They had to come out into the open!

Slowly the two men walked down the deserted street. They looked neither to the right nor left. There was something odd to their walk. As if they were walking tiptoe, expectant of disaster. Then the chapel was before them.

Witson scurried in between the boundary walls of the chapel and the adjoining building. Norton followed.

Their goal proved to be a narrow, squat building.

Witson turned a face that was an odd mixture of weariness and elation in Norton's direction.

"This is it," he said, turning the knob and entering.

"Aye," said a strange voice. "This is it!"

A strangled sound came from Witson's lips.

"Mio!" he gasped.

The man facing them smiled. His lips made a deep V in his face. Norton found time to notice that the V motif was carried out throughout; in the shape of the ears and the way the hair lay. Then Mio spoke again:

"Did you think us fools? We knew all along that you were using this place for a hide-away. So that when you got away from the patrol last night we simply waited here for your return."

Norton didn't have to turn to know that there were men behind them. He heard movement of shod feet on the tile floor. He turned his head casually and saw ten men standing about in watchful attitudes. The door was still open, just as when they had stepped inside. He gave their captors a curious look. It was obvious that they came from a land or place beyond his knowledge.

They we're all dressed alike, in close fitting jackets of some metallic substance. Covering their limbs were skin-tight doublets, the ends of which were tucked into ankle-length boots. Facially, they all looked alike. He noted the absence of interest they showed and thought it odd.

Mio gave an order:

"Truss them up!"

Norton would have attempted to fight. But he saw that several of the men had taken a pistol-like weapon from a holster on their belt. The memory of what had happened to the tree when the charge it contained struck it, still stuck. He remained lax as they bound his arms.

They walked through one of the two halls and out a door leading to a side street. Drawn up at the curb was a strange vehicle. Slim, cigar-shaped, it was about thirty feet long and perhaps ten feet thick.

There were no wheels on the vehicle. A door, set flush into the curved wall, opened and they stepped within. No sooner were they seated than the car started. Norton's eyebrows lifted when he noticed the complete absence of motion. He turned to remark on it to Witson, and Mio said:

"Outside!"

Norton went, "huh?" And one of the guards nudged him heavily. There was no mistaking the implied command. Norton stepped out. They were in front of the city hall.

All seemed confusion. There was a constant parade of armed men coming in and out of the building. The two men were quickly herded through the swinging doors and into an elevator, manned by one of the now familiar outsiders. In the hurried glimpse Norton had of the street, he noticed the fewness of people.

The elevator stopped at the fourth floor and they marched in quick step to an office at the end of the hall. Two men stood to either side of the glass-fronted door. One of them swung the door wide and Norton and Witson followed Mio and two of the others into the office.

A man sat at a side desk. He was the only one in the room.

Mio bowed his head in a sharp nod and said:

"These are the two the guards saw last night."

"Good!" said the man at the desk. "All right you two, step forward."

Norton looked down at the man. He could feel Witson's body tremble as it pressed against his. The man behind the desk said nothing. He looked very much like Mio. And Norton saw then that there was more than a similarity of looks. There was a cruelty to the set of their lips and to the high arch of their eyelids, a cruelty that needed the smallest of excuses only to come into the open. The two looked at each other with the same degree of intensity. Then the man behind the desk said:

"How was it you escaped our patrols on the first night?"

Norton snorted aloud.

"Perhaps because they were too stupid to find me?" he suggested ironically.

THE other's eyelids crinkled in a smile. And Norton went to his knees as one of the guards struck him from behind. Blood trickled from his nostrils. He shook his head, clearing it from the cobwebs of shock and rose to his feet. The smile had reached the other's lips.

"Aren't you going to suggest that I remove your bonds? It seems to be a common complaint among your countrymen that we are bullies and cowards," he said.

Norton smiled a crooked smile. The blood dribbled down and past the corner of his mouth. Passion had boiled in his breast for the barest second, after the blow, but now he was filled with a cold curiosity about these people. Anger and the consequences of it would avail him nothing, he realized.

"I'm afraid you have the wrong man for that," he answered mildly. "Stupidity is not one of my vices."

"Very well put," the other said. "Perhaps we can use you—in a capacity more fitted to your intelligence."

"Perhaps? Would you permit me a small allowance of curiosity?"

"Yes?"

"Why have we been brought here? What is your purpose?"

Norton didn't expect an answer. The other did, however.

"To use you as a laborer. The hidden city will be found and when we have, there must be several hundred thousand of you people put to work. Simple, isn't it?"

"As far as I'm concerned, yes. But why the old man?"

"He was agile enough to lead us a merry chase. Then he's capable of doing labor."

"Since when do the men of Mu use men of science as slaves?" Witson asked unexpectedly.

The man behind the desk stiffened in surprise. His mouth opened loosely then closed in a this lipped vise.

"What do you know of Mu, old fool?" he snapped out sharply.

"As much…" Norton began to explain when the other broke in:

"Be still! Let the old one answer Ribal."

"I know that it still lives," Witson answered.

There was an interval of silence. Then Ribal arose and said:

"Perhaps it were best that Jetto sees the both of you? Follow me."

Ribal waved the two guards and Mio from the room and opened a door, which led to an inner office. They followed him as he went through the room beyond the door and then into a long corridor. At the end of the corridor was another door, this one of plain wood. It was unguarded. Ribal opened it and motioned for the two to go in.

It proved to be just another office. But there were no desks in this one. A long, low couch ran the width of the room. Behind it, Norton caught a glimpse of the building fronting La Salle Street. Drapes made a clear view impossible. There were a half dozen men in the room. They were clustered about the couch and the man sitting on it.

Heads turned at the sound of the door opening. As Ribal and his prisoners advanced, the men parted in front of the man on the couch to give Norton a full view of the important personage.

HE SAW a man of average build. A narrow, triangular beard, started an inch below his lower lip, gave to the man an appearance of intellectuality, a look bore out by the high, though narrow forehead. He was dressed as the rest. There seemed to be no variation to the Murian's manner of dress. There was something about this man, though, that was a little different from the rest. Some inner spirit that showed through the flesh. It showed in his eyes and the cool regard with which he looked them over.

"The reason for this interruption had better be one of importance," he said in a voice that was like a twanging steel wire.

The rest of the Murians listened and looked with cold indifference at the two prisoners.

"Aye, mighty Jetto! Ribal would not disturb the conference, if he didn't—"

"All right, man. Get on with it."

"These two have claim to being men of science."

Norton didn't remember claiming any such distinction for himself. But he let it ride.

The man on the couch looked at the two before him up and down. It was a gesture devoid of interest.

"Hmmm," Jetto murmured in sudden appraisal. "Men of science, eh? Perhaps we can use them, Fu-ta, not that I have changed my mind from its original thought, but from sheer expediency," Jetto threw the words to one of the men standing close to his side.

The one called Fu-ta said, "The Prime Number man in the city they call New York has already sent word that the people there are forming groups of revolt."

Jetto's dark brows drew together in sudden anger.

"Damn them, then!" he keened in a high, passionate voice. "If they interfere, I'll give them more than just a taste of madness. And this time it will not be accidental."

"Jetto, I beg of you. We simply don't have the men with which to war on them. Any delay can be costly."

Jetto's breath whistled from his nostrils in a high, thin sound.

"Very well," he muttered harshly. "You two...do you carry any weight with your people? Will they listen to you?"

Witson answered for them:

"About myself, I can say that I am not well known in any field other than anthropology. But Dale Norton's name is a household word throughout the world."

"So?"

"Yes," Witson went on, "if he has anything to say, the people will listen."

"Good!" Jetto exclaimed. "Now before I give you your instructions, let me first tell you a thing or two. We have no interest in your planet other than what we came here for. That some "things" happened and caused misery and death are a matter of regret. It was a sort of accidental slipping of a gear in our machinery. Who and what we are is no concern of yours..."

"Mind if I put in my two cents?" Norton broke in.

The thin, finely drawn face of the man on the couch broke into lines of anger, but Norton went on as if he did not see it:

"I think it is our concern. We pride ourselves on the fact that liberty, personal and national, is not a cloak that we can wear or not at anyone's discretion. It is part of us, like the flesh and bone of our bodies. And when that liberty has been violated, and in the manner or rather the violent willfulness of your violating, then the people will *demand* an accounting. What were your reasons for what has happened? Why was this violence necessary?"

JETTO controlled himself with an effort that was plain to see. He spoke slowly, measuring each word for effect:

"Very well, Norton. We have come from a far universe, beyond any of your knowledge. Once we lived on this planet. Many thousands of years ago. First in huge underground cities. Then above the ground in great communities. All these cities were colonies, established by some far-sighted ancestor of mine, against the day when his mother planet would no longer support a human population. Nor was this the only planet.

"There was one other, the planet, Pa-Mura. It proved to be the better suited for us. We migrated in huge space ships, both from here and the mother planet to the one they found in outer space. But before the migration was complete, disaster struck. Cataclysms, in the form of floods and earthquakes struck and engulfed these cities.

"Great numbers of people lost their lives. Worse, certain scientific machinery was lost. It is because of that loss that we are here. We must have the machines before we depart."

The two men before Jetto had given him their full attention. He had been aware of that from the very beginning. It was not for nothing that he was known as Jetto the Crafty. It was no longer a man, addressing them, but an actor.

The finely drawn face was mobile in the extreme, changing with every mood. His mouth had drooped when he spoke of the catastrophe that had happened, as if he held a grief for the victims of it. His face became exalted when he spoke of the glories of his mother race. Now, his shoulders and arms lifted in supplication, as he came to the climax, to the clincher in his plea for Norton's help:

"But that is only a minor reason for our being here. Peace has been our constant companion on Pa-Mura. I was at the head of the state. And a gang, understand, a *gang*, seized control of the government while I was away. I had to flee for my life! But I remembered this planet and the colonies it once had. And remembered too the scientific riches they had held. Norton...I know where one of those cities is buried!

"And with your help, we will excavate for it. Neither you nor any of those who help, will be the loser for it. I promise you that."

They were almost convinced of his sincerity. In fact, Witson *was*, so great an actor was Jetto. Not Norton, however. He could not give an explanation for his disbelief. Instinct told him that Jetto had not told all. That there was a part, some small or large distortion to the tale.

"You have answered my questions fairly enough," Norton said. "But I don't understand why you want me. Witson, here, has exaggerated my importance. It may be true, as he says, that my name is a household word, but that does not make me a statesman. We have a president and ruling body in Washington. Certainly they..."

"I am so sorry!" Jetto interrupted. "A most unfortunate and regrettable accident happened. Because we did not know how we would be received, we had to take certain steps to make our landing safe. Your leader and certain high members of his council were in a theater at the time...it was quite horrible. And because those who were in high places did not believe that his, er, accident, was not pre-meditated, they would not cooperate. So you see, we have little choice in the matter of finding a voice to explain our position."

NORTON was aghast at the words. In a theater. He thought of another who had also been a victim of an assassin. And also in a theater. He was about to ask what happened to those who failed to cooperate, when there was an unscheduled interruption.

The double doors, which opened out into the main corridor, swung wildly open and a man ran in, bowing his head in quick jerks as he approached the couch. He panted out the message he had for Jetto:

"Mighty Jetto! The—Prime Number—from New York—enemy craft approaching—wants instructions!"

A terrible change came over Jetto's face. His temper, quick to burn, blazed instantly.

"Use the blast wave on them!" he shouted. "Stupid fools Do they think to stop me? Daring to face me with their childish space ships."

The messenger departed, as he came, bowing and scraping. But before he quite reached the door, Norton stopped him.

"Wait!" he commanded.

The man turned, looking quickly from Norton to his leader.

"That isn't necessary," Norton lowered his voice from a shout to a conversational plane. "Let me talk to them over the radio. Let me…"

"No. I've listened to enough. Both to Fu-ta and you. You'll do as I say. And without reservation."

"And if I don't?" Norton asked darkly.

"Then I'll make you wish you had," Jetto answered. There was that in his voice which made chills run down Norton's back. He had not the slightest doubt that Jetto could and would keep his promise. Yet his answer was the only one he could give.

"Okay, mister," he said. "You can do your damndest. But you won't get this man to play stooge for you."

"And you can count me in on that too," came the high-pitched voice of Witson, in echo.

Jetto's face became scarlet as it filled with blood, so great was his anger. His whole body shook in the grip of it. He pointed a quivering hand at them.

"Take them away," he said venomously. "And put them into the deepest and darkest hole of a prison you can find. And let them rot there until I can think up a torture to fit their crime."

Norton and his friend were passive in the grip of the guards who had appeared as if by magic. This time they were not handled with the care that had been exercised before. They were dragged to the door. But before they were shoved through, Norton turned and laughed full in Jetto's face. It was a small but worthwhile pleasure.

Once again they were put into one of the oddly shaped cars. And once again there was that terrific, speedy ride. It was over in a second. The flush-door opened and they stepped out. Norton recognized the building before them, instantly. It was the old county jail.

CHAPTER THREE

THE dirt-grimed stones were grayness melting into grayness, each a gravestone marker to the years. In the early sixties the health department, which had been using the building, moved into its own. It had remained vacant since then. Now it was a prison once again.

An entire company of Murian warriors was deployed around the structure. Strange looking weapons were mounted at the four corners, evidence of the Murians' fear that the people's will to revolt was not entirely dead. The guards, with Norton and Witson between them, rushed through the doors. They were shoved against a wall, while the leader of the squad reported to his superior.

Most of the Murians Norton had seen were, if not pleasant looking, at least human in features. This man was neither. Something had happened to his face. It was all out of focus. His nose was squashed flat against his cheeks. A great gash had been torn from a cheek and his right eye hung down on the mutilated flesh in an unnerving stare. A sword had bitten deeply across his mouth and as a result it hung askew in an idiot's grin.

This was Tomet, their jailer!

He regarded them malevolently for several seconds without saying anything. His right hand toyed with the stock of a lash that hung from the belt around his waist. His inspection over, he said:

"Ntho they nwon't cooperate, neh? N'nhen pwaps I c'n ndo nsomething nabout nthat."

Witson burst into a cackle of laughter and even Norton had to smile. Tomet had the body of a man, but the voice was that of a woman. And a woman with a bad lisp.

Tomet's one good eye went wide at the unexpected sound. Then the lids squeezed tight over it and with a high-pitched shriek of rage he charged at them, pulling as he ran, at the lash hanging from the belt. It came free as he skidded to a halt before them.

"Nthere!" he shrieked, as he savagely swung the single thong across Witson's face and shoulders. "Nthere—nah—nah—nah." His voice held nothing human in it.

For the barest instant Norton was stood immobile, as if he were spellbound by the savagery of the attack. Then he leaped to the defense of his friend. Tomet's blows had been wanton and cruel. Norton's were deliberate, cold and even more savage. For they were scientific and struck in a manner to give the most hurt without making the victim lose consciousness.

Tomet was a big man but he was dwarfed by Norton who stood several inches over six feet. The scientist struck pile driver blows, deliberately twisting his fist as it struck into the features of the jailer. Tomet's face was lacerated and torn open.

A phalanx of bodies struck Norton. The guards had come to Tomet's rescue. It was not unexpected. Even as Norton went to Witson's defense, he had taken into account the fact that he had at the most only a few seconds in which to inflict whatever damage he could. Nor was he unaware of the consequences that might occur as a result of his action. It had not swayed him in the slightest degree.

Witson went to his knees from a blow of a club in the hands of one of the guards. Norton stepped protectingly before him and dealt out punishment by means of his fists.

But it was an unequal fight. The guards had clubs and there were twenty of them pitted against him. One of them stepped back and flung his club. It struck Norton across the bridge of the nose, blinding him with pain. His arms went up in a reflexive movement to protect his eyes and in that instant the rest of the guards piled on. While some pinioned his arms, others struck with fists and clubs.

NORTON went to his knees, slowly, as a mighty tree falls. Nor did they stop beating at him, even then. It was Tomet, oddly enough, who stopped the slaughter:

"Nwait!" he shrieked. "Jetto nwants him nalive."

They jerked him roughly erect. His head hung low, chin resting against his chest. He hung laxly between the two men who held him, blood dripping in a steady stream from the cuts on his forehead and cheek. He was numb with pain. They dragged him off. Nor was he more than dimly aware of what they were doing.

"Ho, 7," one of his guards called.

Norton lifted his head at the sound of the voice.

His pain-filled eyes took in their surroundings, but in the distorted focus of one in a dream. Then the focus sharpened, his nose became aware of an odor, and his senses awakened.

He shook himself free of the restraining grips of the guards. They stepped back, their hands flying to the clubs in their belts. But he wasn't interested in them. Witson lay on the floor beside him. He went to one knee and felt with probing fingers for the pulse. It beat, but feebly. And all the while he was bent, feeling for the spark of life in Witson's body, all his senses were aware of the horrible odor all about him. It was the foul, decaying odor of human flesh, too long in confinement and without any of the ordinary means of relief. It was as fetid and miasmic as the air from some malarial swamp.

"What's wrong here?" a new voice rasped.

Norton lifted his head and measured the man he saw. If it was number 7, he was not a prepossessing sight. He was short and squat, with a barrel chest and arms that hung to his knees. His eyes were Mongoloid and even in the dimness of the passage, Norton saw the cruelty lying in their depths.

"They got a little rough with Tomet," one of the guards offered in explanation.

"Hmmm. So they're a couple of tough birds, eh? Well, two of my little birds in the third cage got sick yesterday and we had to give them a bath, in the river. That makes it just right. The cages got to be full, you know," he said and roared in laughter. He sobered up quickly and gave a command:

"Well...don't stand there like a pair of idiots. Throw them in..."

"Wait." Norton said quietly.

"Huh?" 7 said.

"This man needs a doctor," Norton said.

"Naw... Now ain't that too bad. Maybe he just needs a change of air. *Doctor!* Throw them in three cell," 7 roared.

"Jetto won't like it," Norton said slowly.

There was a second's silence.

"Go on," 7 said.

"He wants us kept alive. And I can assure you that if this man doesn't get medical attention, he'll die."

7 looked to the two guards who nodded their heads vigorously in affirmation.

"Well, why didn't you idiots say so?" he bellowed. "Let's see," he said cocking his head to one side in thought. "Where'll we put them? Ah...I've got it. That end cell's only got one man in it. That traitor. Carry the old guy in there."

THE stench was so great, Norton breathed in shallow gasps, as they walked the length of the corridor, past the rows of cells on either side. Shrieks, groans and curses followed them in their march. The poor wretches in the cells gave voice to their hatred as best they could. The guards, Norton noticed, walked as quickly as they could even though there wasn't the slightest chance that they would be harmed.

Norton took the body of the semiconscious Witson from them as one of them inserted the key 7 had given him into the lock. The door opened on creaking, rusty hinges. He carried the old man across the threshold and the door slammed closed. There was a slatted heavy bench on either side of the room. Norton put the figure of Witson on it.

He had been aware of a strange sound in the cell, when they came in. It was the sound of a voice humming a tune. The sound emanated from the other bench, which was at the other end of the cell. He peered closely toward it and saw a figure reclining on it.

"Mind giving me a hand, here?" Norton asked.

The figure arose and came slowly forward. It was a Murian. He came and stood beside Norton who was engaged in removing Witson's outer garments. Norton threw him a glance over his shoulder. He saw a fairly tall man, slenderly built but of a ranginess that suggested hidden strength. He could not see his face clearly in the gloomy light. Then the man bent forward to look more closely at Witson and Norton saw that the stranger was young. More, that there was intelligence, humor and strength in his features.

"Hmmm. Doesn't look too good," the stranger said. "7 better get the doctor here in a hurry."

Witson's breath, which had been coming in shallow gasps, now had a rattling quality to it. It was obvious that he had been badly hurt. Norton forgot his own pain and wounds.

"Damn them!" he gritted through tight lips. "Where's that doctor?"

"Here, here," a voice answered in frightened tones. "Be with you in a second."

The door swung open and a man scuttled into the cell. 7's voice followed him in:

"And see to it that he lives, understand?"

"Don't worry," the doctor said in pleading tones. "I will."

The physician moved across the dank cell toward Witson.

"Oh dear!" the doctor exclaimed in a frightened tone. "Why don't they have lights so a man can see what he's doing." The fright in his voice was only part of the greater fright that possessed every part of him.

Silence answered his query. They could hear 7's footsteps slapping down the corridor.

The doctor was a frightened, little man, emaciated from hunger, whose thin face was covered with a stubble of beard. His eyes leaped from one to another in the cell in silent begging for understanding. Almost gently, Norton said:

"You're with friends. Don't be afraid."

"They were all my friends," the doctor said tearfully. "Now…"

Norton arose and patted the thin shoulders. The thin frame shuddered under Norton's reassuring fingers, then stiffened, abruptly.

"I'm all right now," the doctor said. "Thanks."

Norton watched the thin, strong fingers at work. The doctor kneaded and prodded at Witson, eliciting a moan of pain, now and then. The doctor shook his head, in silent reproach.

"If only there was more light," he said softly.

NORTON thrust his hands into the pockets of his trousers. He knew that in a second more he would begin hammering at the walls in futile anger. Slowly, he withdrew one of his hands. Clenched within it was a paper pad, of matches.

"Will these help?" he asked.

"Yes, yes," the doctor replied excitedly. "One at a time, though. We may need them all."

He was right. To the last match. When the doctor arose, there were new lines of tiredness around his mouth. But in his eyes there was triumph.

"He'll live," he said in a low voice. "I'll give him something to ease the pain and put him to sleep for a while."

He picked up the case from which he had taken several vials of pills and a hypodermic needle. Norton, a close observer, saw that frightened as he had been, the doctor was a thorough man. He had given Witson as complete an examination as was possible under the circumstances. The doctor pulled the stopper from one of the small bottles and inserted the needle within, drawing out a small quantity of the drug it contained. He shot the whole amount into Witson's arm.

"A combination of penicillin and neoscadrine," he explained. "Lucky I had some left. It'll take care of both the shock and wounds, the latter of which are not of importance, let me assure you. However, the shock is. He's not young, you know."

Norton was only half-listening. His eyes were riveted on the case. He had seen another needle in it.

"Er, doctor?"

"Yes?"

"Suppose something comes up? And you won't be here, of course. Mind if I have one of those needles?"

The doctor regarded him silently for several seconds, then smiled.

"But of course," he replied. "I understand. Here take one. You know how to use it?"

"Yes."

"Good…and here. A vial of this will prove to be of help, also."

Norton waited until the doctor had left under the escort of one of the guards before he opened his palm. The small vial in his palm was marked, morphine.

"Think you'll be able to use it?" the Murian asked.

Norton shrugged his shoulders. Now that the problem of Witson was solved, he felt he was able to give his full attention to this stranger from another planet.

"Am I right in thinking that, er, you are considered a traitor?" he asked.

The other smiled pleasantly and said: "So they say. And rightly."

"What happened?"

"Well, being a prime number, I was in charge of the landing in this area. An order came through to use a certain ray. I refused. That was all."

"What is this prime number business?" Norton asked. There was more than curiosity in his question. If this man was a rebel, then they had gained an ally. His question was his opening wedge to gain the other's confidence.

"Sorry," the other said in a pleasant tone. "Of course you don't know. You see, I'm a mutation. So is 7. And any one of us who has a number instead of a name."

"Let me get this straight," Norton said in an incredulous tone. "You are a *manufactured* being?"

"That's right."

"But you are flesh and blood."

"I might as well explain," the other said, moving to his bench and sitting down. "Here, sit by me. Your friend will be all right."

CHAPTER FOUR

NORTON glanced at Witson and saw that he was under the influence of the drug the doctor had administered. The Murian made himself comfortable, drew one leg up on the bench and rested his chin against the knee.

"You've got to remember," he began, "that they were an old civilization when this very planet was young. And there were wise men among them. The race was dying. Their culture was dying. And so the wise men decreed that before they died out altogether, it was best that they find another planet on which to settle. But with whom? And for what posterity?

"It was a problem that had to be settled before the migration began. We were the solution. So we were born. Fathered by a chemical formula and mothered by a test tube. It is said that there were millions of us here. There are still millions on Pa-Mura. And that is how we are thought of, as a number, into the millions."

"Incredible," Norton whispered softly. "But you are— it would be impossible to tell you from…"

"Except for one basic, organic difference," the Murian said. "And with one problematical, religious difference, we are as human as you. We cannot reproduce. And being manmade, we have no soul."

"Soul?" Norton drew back in surprise. The thought that these people had religious concepts or rather whether they had a philosophical concept of a soul had not occurred to him.

It was as if the Murian had read his mind.

"Why not?" he asked. "We had been given a mind. A mind that functioned. Therefore certain mysteries of concept of morals presented themselves and begged for an answer. It was then we discovered that we had no soul. For in the questions of evil and right, they proved to be words barren of meaning. Machines, whether they are of metal or flesh, have no reason for existence beyond their immediate use. And when they are worn out, they can be discarded without any thought for their future. At least that was the condition until, oh, twenty years or so ago. I was the one responsible for the change. And that is the reason I am here."

Norton's brain whirled from the impact of the Murian's words. Questions, which once had been burning issues and because there was no one to answer them, had died, might now be answered. He listened, as a child, hearing the wonders of *Alice in Wonderland* for the first time.

"It was a woman who was responsible for the whole thing," the other went on. "Beautiful as a childhood dream. Wondrous as the birth of a new day. She," he sighed in the memory of his lost dream, "awakened in me a something that had never been known by any of us before. Love... Surprised?" he asked as Norton murmured an inaudible something. "Don't you understand? There can't be love without a soul from which to stem. Something, perhaps the great Creator, had finally taken pity upon us, or perhaps...but there's no use in idle speculation. At any rate, she reciprocated my feelings. And because it would have been death to have shown our love openly, we were clandestine in our meetings. We couldn't get married. But listen, Earthman, there is a man-child up there on Pa-Mura and he is mine, and some day I shall go back to him.

"I think that I was the first to have realized what happened. Maybe it occurred to all of us mutations at the same time? But in the space of a second, a condition that had existed for eons no longer held. A soul had been granted us. I told you that there were wise men on that planet.

"They realized the change as quickly as we and reasoned out the cause. We were granted full liberty to do as we wished. If it hadn't been for Jetto!"

"Ah," Norton said softly. "The villain enters."

"YES," the Murian said. And Norton saw the grin on his face.

It was not the sort of grin that held humor, however. Rather it was like some grimace, which from torture twisted his lips into the semblance of a smile.

"Yes," the Murian reiterated. "The villain entered. Jetto the crafty, ruler of the chief city, Pa-Mura. Vain, filled with a consciousness of his power, a treacherous man, who was said to have gained his rule through treachery, he hated the thought of giving us freedom. So he evolved a grand scheme of revolt.

"To the great number of us mutations, a new way of life had been opened. There were moral reasons for our actions. But to some, and I cannot say why, there was no change at all. Jetto attempted to organize these into a band, which would openly rebel against those in authority. There were a great number of them and it might have succeeded. But he wanted all the mutations to be part of the revolt.

"We not only refused but went to the Great Council and told them of his plan. War had not been known on Pa-Mura for a long time. And the weapons they had were terrible in their effects. They debated what to do. And Jetto, learning he had been betrayed, struck first. He almost succeeded in doing what he wanted. But there were too many against him. So he took those who were allied with him and using almost the entire space navy of Pa-Mura, set out for this planet. He vowed he would return and obliterate Pa-Mura with the weapons he would bring with him. But now I wonder."

"About what?"

"Whether he will return. If he finds what he set out to, there will be none who could stand up to him here. And I think that will please him more than having to go back there and take the chance of fighting and maybe not winning."

A faint snore interrupted their talk. Witson had fallen into a natural sleep. The noises of the other prisoners had died down. The two in the cell seemed to be the only ones alive in all the prison. And Norton had the oddest feeling that they too were dead. The dead speaking of the dead in hushed whispers, as if it would have made any difference had they shouted. Norton didn't think for a single second that Jetto intended to let them go free.

"*If he finds...* I thought he knew," Norton asked.

"Only the general location. I am the only one who knows the specific point. That was why he kidnapped me."

"For the love of heaven, man! Don't dawdle so..." Norton broke off in exasperation.

"Sorry," the other murmured. "You see, since the time of our incubation, we have had our paths chosen for us. Mine was science. By I matured, I knew what I wanted. Ethnology, the study of man. I attained honors and was made head of the department at our highest university. As such, I had charge of all the records of the expeditions that our peoples had made to other planets. Jetto knew that. What he didn't know, was that I wouldn't tell. So I am here. And no matter what he intends to do, I still won't tell."

"Ethnology, eh? Well, Witson and you will have good a time," Norton said reflectively. "He's got some odd ideas, that will probably interest you. But what I want to know, is what made you land in such places as this city and others of like importance?"

"Oh that," the Murian passed it off lightly. "Our space ships are equipped with devices that enabled us to see, long before we were even close, what the situation was like here. Jetto planned a landing and the use of the ray to inflict as many casualties as was possible. Then too, the after effect of the ray he used makes people lethargic and easily led. Each of your large cities had a quota of men assigned to it."

"I think I've got the whole picture, now," Norton said. "His idea was to kill off as many as he could. Then take advantage of the panic, which was bound to ensue. Before the people could recover their senses, he was in control. But I don't get what he wants?"

"Power," was the answer. "He's had it for a long time. It doesn't make any difference over whom. It's just the idea. *He* wants to have power about everything. And if he gets to the Bad Lands of Utah, he will have that power."

"Is that where the buried city is located?"

"Yes."

NORTON whistled shrilly through his teeth, a habit of his boyhood days.

"That is the reason," the Murian went on, "why we landed on this part of the continent. We observed that the greater part of the population lived to the east of a large river..."

"The Mississippi," Norton interjected.

"...it was obvious then, that we had to gain control of that section of the country."

Norton moved away from the other and sat at his ease, leaning back against the wall. The Murian watched him for a moment, then seeing that Norton wanted to be alone in his thoughts, moved off, to stand against the bars of their cell.

The Murian turned at the sound of a sigh from Norton.

"What of yourself and your friend? How did you incur the enmity of Jetto?"

Norton related what had happened to him and closed with:

"So I guess that we are in the same boat. And from appearance sake, I'd say the boat had an awfully large leak."

"You mean this prison? Remember that we have the needle the doctor gave you. And that one guard looks like another. Tell me, was it still daylight when you were brought here?"

"Y-yes," Norton replied. "Why?"

"Because I am of the opinion that the night is about ended. I know how to operate one of our destroyers. All we have to do is get free. That's where the needle comes in."

"I don't get it," Norton was puzzled.

The Murian grinned broadly and lay down at full length on the bench. A series of horrible groans came from his lips. Norton's lips twisted in a smile. He knew what the other was driving at.

"Guard!" he shouted. "Guard! Help, quick. This man's dying."

There was a few seconds silence. Then other prisoners became aware of Norton's continuing shouts. A cacophony of shrieks, groans, curses and screams filled the air. Then there was the voice of the guard shouting for silence. And above all the other sounds was heard the stentorian voice of Norton, still calling for help.

Norton heard the guard approach and ran back to the bench on which the other lay, doubled up in such a way that his back was to whoever made an examination.

The cell door squealed open. A hand descended on Norton's shoulder, pushing him to one side. The guard knelt and tried to pull the stricken man over to where he could see what was wrong. And as he knelt, Norton inserted the needle into the small vial the doctor had left with him. When he withdrew it the needle was full of a whitish substance. He turned to see if the guard had come alone. He had.

Norton's right hand went around the guard's mouth and before the man knew what had happened, the needle had gone in for its entire length into the jugular vein. Norton held him for the space of a minute. When he released him, the guard slumped to the floor. His body had barely touched the floor when the Murian was tearing at his clothes and handing them to Norton.

The last thing he took was the guard's belt and a small metallic something which resembled a water pistol.

"Now," the Murian said, as Norton finished dressing. "I defy anyone to tell the difference. Here's what we do. I'll carry the old man. You'll follow close behind. Be sure that you hold the gun close to my back, for realism sake. Only keep your hand from the trigger. The corridor is dark enough so that there won't be much chance of anyone guessing what happened. There's a barred door at the head of the stairs. At this hour, I don't think more than one man will be at the door. I'll stall him for a moment. Stay close behind. If he shows the slightest suspicion press on the trigger. It'll blast him straight to hell. From then on we're on our own. Let's go!"

NORTON heard the sound of the prisoner's catcalls all the way up the stairs. He concentrated on hearing them. And when they made the turn into the last landing, he was sorry that he could no longer hear them. For from here on he knew that reality might be only a figment of his imagination. Then the steel bars of the last door between them and freedom stood before them.

At the sound of their approaching footsteps, a man arose from a low stool on which he had been taking his ease.

"Who goes?" he asked, yawning broadly as if the answer was a foregone conclusion. But it was a formula, which had to be gone through.

"This man—he is ill, dying," Norton's cellmate answered.

Norton, pressing close to the other, saw the guard's eyes go wide as he recognized first, Witson, then the man carrying him.

"Where's his friend?" he demanded.

"The guard wouldn't let him come," the Murian said. "Said it would be too hard to watch us both."

As the guard stepped forward to open the door, Norton moved to one side, so that the guard couldn't see him. It wasn't until they were all in the enclosure that the keeper realized something was wrong. The Murian, with Witson in his arms, had continued walking to the head of the short flight of stairs leading to the upper part of the prison. Norton continued to avert his head, as he went past the keeper. It was that which made him suddenly suspicious.

"Wait a minute, you!" he called.

When they continued without heeding his command, he ran after them and grabbed Norton by an arm. It was his last act. Norton turned and blasted him with the gun. There was a blinding flash of white light from the muzzle, a light that ended in the keeper's throat. His mouth opened and his eyes went wide. Then he buckled at the knees and toppled slowly forward on his face.

"There's a rear to this building, isn't there?" the Murian asked quickly.

"Yes," Norton answered, assuming the lead.

He made off at a run for the stairs. But not the ones before them. There was another series he knew of that were around the bend and past the desk, which used to house the lock-up keeper. At the head of those stairs was a narrow passage, which in turn led to a steel door, the freight door.

The Murian panted behind him, Witson's still slumbering body bobbing up and down in the man's arms.

Norton took the stairs, three at a time. But he came to an abrupt halt at the head. There was a bisecting corridor to be transversed before they could reach the safety of the alley. He threw up a hand in warning and the Murian panted to a stop beside him. Then he heard what had brought Norton to a halt.

It was the sound of approaching footsteps, marching in the regular rhythm of soldier's steps.

"Damn!" the Murian muttered. "The changing of the guard."

He was right. A file of men stepped smartly into view. There were eight of them in a column of twos. At their head marched one who was their leader, for he was marking time in a low, cadence count. And before the three at the head of the stairs could retreat, they were seen. The guard's surprise was the greater.

Norton didn't wait to see what would happen. He let go once more with the deadly weapon in his hand. Again there was the blinding spurt of white light. Only this time Norton held the trigger down constantly and used the gun in a spray effect. It was terrible in effect. They were as the blades of grass before the steel teeth of the lawn mower. And when he released the trigger, there were only parts of bodies on the floor. The power of the light was fantastic. Whatever it struck was simply consumed as by a holocaust. Norton's gorge rose as he smelled the odor, which came to meet them when they ran past the bodies of the guards.

The door was unlocked. It took a second to lift it. Nor did they worry that it squealed in the process. Safety was too close.

They stood motionless for a moment, breathing in great gulps of the chilly night air.

"What—what happened?" a shrill voice asked.

Witson had finally come out of his drugged sleep.

The Murian set him on his feet. He swayed weakly for a second or two, then recovered quickly. Witson was an old man but there was something of steel in his body, the way he took his knocks and came back for more.

"We'll explain later," Norton said, as he peered up and down the alleyway. He knew that there wasn't much time. The bodies of the men he had killed might be discovered at any moment.

"Come," the Murian said. "I know the way from here."

His pace was slower this time, as if he expected that they might meet someone. And men running in the early hours of the morning are targets of suspicious looks. They couldn't afford to be stopped.

A street lamp shed a feeble glow over the barren street. Dawn was but an hour away. The Murian gave the seemingly empty street a thorough going over with his eyes before he permitted then to venture past the alley mouth. And then not before he gave them final instructions.

"Listen carefully now," he said. "Our destroyer fleet is parked on the lake front. Give me an hour's time. Then meet me at the monument of the Indian horsemen."

He was just another shadow on the street, as he sidled along. Then he was part of the darkness.

AT THAT very moment Jetto was giving his final instructions for the Murian conquest of the United States. His cruel eyes looked contemptuously at the men gathered about him in the huge office.

"I am done with talk!" his voice shrilled at them. "Especially yours, Fu-ta. Who can oppose us? And if they do, they'll get the same dose I meted out to the fools who came to stick their noses into our affairs."

"I don't think that will be the last of them, Jetto," Fu-ta said softly.

"No? Well, if there will be more, they too will get the same reception."

"What of the people here?" Fu-ta demanded.

Jetto, who had been pacing back and forth before the councilors, whirled at the words. They shrank from the look of fury in his face. All but Fu-ta.

"I will do with them as I did with the two who were here earlier. Worse. I will make this the land of the damned for them. And that reminds me, Prime Number 1, is down there. Another who thinks to defy me. Wait until I tell him of his child: it will do me good to see the knave's face when I tell him what will happen if he doesn't do as I say."

"Jetto!" Fu-ta's voice suddenly rang out. "The die has been cast. We chose to come with you. But this is not Pa-Mura. We are on foreign soil. And but a handful among enemies. You have scattered our forces over a large area. Bring them here…"

Jetto bit his lips in vexation. Fu-ta was right. Fu-ta was always right! Some day the man would have to be removed. Already some of the others were begging to question him also. A benign smile made its way to his mouth.

"Did Fu-ta think I was going to let them stay there till eternity?" he asked with a sweetness that was a cutting rebuke to the man who dared to question his judgment. "That damned mutation will give in, mark my words, and when he does, we will go out to the hidden spot. But first I must recruit the labor."

"You won't do it by having the ones who *can* do it for you, thrown into jail," Fu-ta said.

Ganto, the scribe, looked up at the words. He had been an interested spectator to the play between the two men.

"If we don't stop killing them off, soon there won't be enough of them to build a hut," he said in his gentle, unobtrusive way.

"What do you mean?" Jetto asked.

"The ray we loosed on them accounted for more than half the population. When we were forced to use the blast power on them, we killed off another third. And since we were indiscriminate in the use of our force, many were killed who could have been put to use."

Jetto's eyes rolled in his head. These mites and their way of looking at trifles. As if it mattered whether he killed off the whole population. That would make everything simple, then. Didn't they know yet, that he had no intention of returning to Pa-Mura.

"All right," he said in resignation. "What do you want me to do?"

"There isn't much you can do, I'm afraid," Ganto said. "But let us make some sort of arrangement with them for good will. Those two who were here this afternoon. Call them back. Let us talk to them."

"Very well," Jetto said in agreement.

TOMET the jailer yawned broadly. Damn them anyway! The nerve of it—waking a man from a sound sleep. Didn't they ever go to bed? He looked angrily at the messenger, who returned the look with one of indifference.

"Ought to ghet nhrid of nhe thcum," he grunted, as he got to his feet. "'nstead of nputting nthem in nhail. Nhmmm. Nmaybe 'hat's what Njetto whants to nhdo, eh?"

The messenger shrugged his shoulders.

Tomet gave him a sour look and proceeded to shuffle off down the stairs, which led to the cells. The messenger sat down in the vacant chair and waited for his return. It wasn't long.

Tomet literally erupted from the stairs. His misshapen face was grey, his eyes stared in wild disbelief and his twisted mouth twitched.

"Gone—gone!" he babbled hysterically. "All three. And the guards. blasted! The whole lot of them!"

The messenger didn't wait to hear any more. Swiftly, he turned and ran from the room.

CHAPTER FIVE

Number 1 peered cautiously around the corner of the building. The street was empty of life. His eyes narrowed in speculation. He knew too well the risk he was taking. And the consequences of being caught. But in that low, walled building across the way were a dozen men who would join him at a word. And he needed them badly.

A sentry walked across the path of his vision. And a broad grin spread across the watcher's face. It was double 7. The sentry whirled at the whispered sound, which came to him from across the still-dark street. His fingers toyed restlessly with the blast pistol in his hand. Then he recognized the man who stepped out from the darkened doorway and a look of incredulous disbelief spread across his features. Quickly, he ran to the other and embraced him in greeting.

"I—I thought—why we were told that Jetto had executed you," he said.

"Fah!" the other replied. "You know Jetto. That would have been the sensible thing to do. But not he. Torture first. So this little bird flew the coop. But tell me, are our friends still with us?"

Double 7 went wide-eyed at the question.

"But of course," he said in a hurt voice, as if he was surprised that the other should even ask such a thing.

Number one sighed in relief. "Good!" he exclaimed. Then he gave orders as though it was the natural thing to do and not as if he was a hunted man. "We can't work in half measures now, things are coming to a head, I'm sure.

And I've got to beat Jetto to the punch. Go back to the barracks and tell Number 9 to follow through with the plan we conceived. Kill all those who are not with us and don't have any qualms about killing them. Then get several patrol cars and meet me at the space port on the lake front."

The other had been following Number 1 intently. When his leader finished, the sentry turned and left without a further word. "Stay here," Number 1 said to Norton. "I'll be right back."

THE Loop was dark. Darker than Norton had ever remembered it being. And quiet. With the unearthly quiet of a thing dead, yet having life. They were but two more shadows among the many of the street.

A patrol car came around the corner and the two men melted into the shadows of a building's entrance. A headlight swept across the panes of glass. Then the car passed from view. The two came into the open again.

"Do you mean to tell me," Norton asked, halting their progress momentarily for his question, "that they have so enslaved the people in the two weeks since they've been here, that they are afraid to come out at night?"

"It would be instant death for anyone," Witson said.

Norton shuddered. His mind had pictured once again the scenes of carnage he had come across. If they could only get to the coast? The Murian *had* to get to his friends!

Another car made its presence known. Again they flattened themselves against a wall. And again they remained undetected.

"Who is this man who has gone for help?" Witson asked.

Norton told him what had happened while he was unconscious. They continued their stealthy advance while Norton talked. At the end of his tale, they found themselves facing the broad stretch of Michigan Boulevard. The Mestrovic monument was directly across from them. Norton gave the thoroughfare a hurried glance. It was deserted. Motioning with his head for Witson to follow, he started across the street—and one of the patrol cars turned the corner of the next street.

The two men were caught full in the headlights of the car.

Norton ran full speed for the far curb. But *before* he got there, he heard a moaning cry behind him. Turning his head, he saw that Witson had stumbled to his knees. And saw too, that the car was bearing down on the fallen man. Whirling, he ran back to Witson. He ran bent low, like a football player with the ball. When he got to Witson, he bent and without losing speed caught him up in his arms.

There was a screeching sound from a few feet away and Norton turned a horrified face in the direction of the sound. The car was almost on them. Suddenly there was a blinding flash of light. And hard on its heels there came the sound of an explosion and Norton spun around in the wake of the concussion, but even as he fell, he twisted his body around so that it was protecting Witson.

"Are you all right, my friend?" a voice asked.

Norton turned his head. The gray, dawning light showed him who it was. The Murian! Norton rolled away from Witson, who was muttering profanely. He felt himself all over.

"Y-yes. I think so," Norton replied. He looked over to his fallen friend. "How are you Witson?"

"Like the football at the bottom of a pileup, a little flattened but none the worse from wear," the chippery little man said, arising and dusting himself.

Norton followed the other's example, looking curiously about him as he did so. The patrol car was a mass of twisted, blackened wreckage. Three torpedo-shaped cars were lined up at the curb. The ugly snouts of strange looking guns protruded from open ports in the sides of the cars.

"Good!" the Murian exclaimed in relief. "Let's go, then. We haven't much time. Jetto knows that we have escaped."

The name was a spur to their feet. Quickly they followed the Murian to the car. He made room for them on the wide seat. Three men sat beside the driver.

"Lucky for you my men spotted me as I was walking along," he said. "They would never have stopped otherwise. And of course I recognized you both."

"Lucky so far," Norton reminded him. "Let's hope our luck will hold out."

"I see you still have the blast pistol," the Murian said, looking down at the belt around Norton's waist. "We'll need more than luck from here in. We're going in shooting. Better stick close to my side."

THE driver had turned the car until it faced the grassy parkway on the east side of the street. Then he let out the throttle and he zoomed across the park. In a matter of seconds, they were at the wire enclosure that barred the huge airstrip that had been constructed at the foot of Congress Street. The other cars pulled up behind them and grim-faced, silent men piled out to form a group about Norton's friend.

"When we get to the gate," the Murian said. "Number 4 will take the lead. If it's barred we'll have to blast it down. If not—then watch me and do as I do."

They nodded in silent agreement.

The first faint rose-colored streaks of dawn tinged the east as they arrived at the gate. It wasn't barred. A sentry leaned somnolently against the gate. He gave them a cursory glance as they passed him. He didn't notice that they weren't all dressed alike. The last man through, slowed down and walked back to the sentry. Norton turned to see what happened. He saw only the faintest streak of light, as the sentry stiffened, then fell to the ground.

To the right, about a hundred yards off, the control tower gleamed in a sudden, rosy reflection of light. Norton detected a faint movement on its serrated top. Now their movements quickened. Ahead he saw the gleaming shapes of huge space ships. Interspersed among them were the smaller, more sleek-looking ones that were the destroyers.

A voice came rumbling down at them from the control tower:

"Halt!"

They paid no attention to the voice.

"Halt or I blast!" the rumbling voice warned.

Norton's lips tightened. He couldn't see the man who was doing the shouting. It was all too evident that they were at his mercy. But the band of ten moved on.

The white glare of a spotlight came swinging around in their direction. It was the signal for pandemonium to break loose.

A group of men burst from the control tower. Another group came running from the far corner of the airport, where there was a building, which in ordinary times, had housed the personnel of the field. And between the racing groups were the parked goals of the space ships.

"Let them have it!" Number 1 shouted as he broke into a run.

In a second the field was crisscrossed by searching fingers of white lights, which held death for anyone caught in their beams. Ahead of him, Norton saw a man fall, to lie in a tortured, twisted heap. Something made him look up to the tower once more. He saw a man wheeling a massive shape onto a platform. He didn't need more than one glance to know that it was a piece of artillery. Forgetting all else, Norton let the others run on as he knelt and took careful aim at the figure on the parapet.

He watched with a spellbound interest, as the beam of light went up from the muzzle of his pistol. He saw the stones crumble when the light struck the edge of the parapet. The light crept higher in a race with the man, who seemed to be having trouble with the field piece. Just as it reached him, he moved behind the gun. The light struck the gun. There was a tremendous blast of sound and the gun, man and entire roof of the tower went up in a flash of flame.

Then Norton arose and raced for the ship that was their goal. Already Number 1 had reached it. In a few seconds they had all scrambled through its door. Norton panted to a stop and a hand reached out and literally lifted him through the hatchway. It clanged shut behind him.

Seven men sat in attitudes of exhaustion on a long bench, which ran the length of the ship. The eighth was at the helm of the ship. Norton's suddenly quivering legs dragged themselves to the bench. He sat there for several minutes, gasping in long, shallow breaths. Beside him, Witson sat and stared through the glassed-in ports. There was something so odd in his expression that Norton followed his glance.

They should have been in bright sunlight. Instead, only the pitch black of outer space met his look. Yet he hadn't even known that they had started, so smooth was the take off. The man at the helm turned his head and said:

"All right, men, man the blast-guns!"

Instantly, those who had been sitting, seemingly so exhausted that it appeared as if nothing could make them move, leaped to their feet.

"There," one of them said, pointing to a seat set into the wall of the ship, "is a gun. Make yourself fast, because this ship is going to go through an awful lot of movement. Press the trigger on the gun in jerks. And shoot at anything that comes in range."

The gun mount reminded Norton of the ones set into the jet propelled planes he had made for the government. Beyond that, there was a vast difference in the crafts. This one had blinding speed. He couldn't understand how the pilot managed maneuvers at such a pace.

OF THOSE who had come into the ship, only Witson remained seated. The rest were at the guns. Norton looked through the aperture before him. He saw the ship's nose was pointed downward. The Earth and ship approached each other at a speed, which dizzied him. Then the pilot flattened the ship out and Norton saw the field, directly below.

He pressed at the trigger, but too late. They had already passed it. The others had not been so slow. In the single glance he had before the plane passed, he saw the parked planes dissolve into rubble, saw huge craters open in the ground. And again there was the transition from light to pitch-blackness.

"Norton!" a voice called.

He turned and saw the pilot motioning him forward.

"Sit here," the other said when Norton reached him.

Norton took the seat. Before him stretched a wide, curving glass, which gave him a clear view of everything in front. It curved to such a degree, in fact that he was even permitted a downward view. The Earth was a huge ball, radiating a beautiful silvery light.

"Listen," the pilot said. "There's a small chance that we might wreck every plane on the field, before they have a chance to send up help for them. Think we ought to take a chance?"

"No!" Norton replied instantly. "Head for the coast. If we can make it there, I think I can organize things to give Jetto a plenty hot reception, when and if he gets to the Bad Lands."

The Murian nodded his head in slow agreement.

"That makes sense," he said. "But let's see what the rest think of the plan."

He did something to the controls, turned and called to the rest who crowded around the two in the pilots' compartment.

"The Earthman speaks sense," he said in conclusion. "At best we can only wreck the ships on this field. If we can reach his friends he feels that they will be able to do something. I leave it to you."

They fell in with Norton's suggestion instantly. For the most part they were young, eager faced men, the stamp of adventure high on their foreheads. But there were two there, who were older. One of these snapped his fingers suddenly. And Norton saw his face take on a pallor at odds with its naturally ruddy complexion.

"I—I forgot in the excitement. Number 1, there is something you must know. Your son…"

The color fled the pilot's face.

"Wh—what…" his voice broke. "What of my son?"

"Jetto has him," the other said.

A look of horror came alive on the pilot's face at the other's words. He opened his mouth but the words would not come.

"I meant to tell you before," the older man said, compassion deep in his tone. "He knew how you felt about his revolt. And so he kidnapped the boy just before we sailed. It was his trump card over you, and I think he will use it."

Number 1, sitting in the pilot's seat, knew exactly what that meant.

"I swear," he said slowly and in a voice that held no sign of emotion, "that if he harms a single lock of the child's hair that I will come back and tear out his heart—with my bare hands!"

He turned and looked for a long moment into the faces of those pressed around him. Then he said:

"We go to seek Norton's friends."

THEY turned and went back to their places at the guns. Only Norton saw the other's face twist in hidden grief. There was nothing he could say—or do. He peered through the window—anything, so that he would not have to look at the other—and saw a silver streak pass them, a silver streak that suddenly glowed red.

The pilot must have seen it too, for he suddenly called, "Guns! Quick! 'Fore they blast us."

The ship was suddenly rocked from stem to stern. Norton was thrown against the instrument panel as the pilot heeled the ship over in a sudden maneuver. Then he stood it on its nose and gave it full throttle. Norton wiped the blood from his nose and watched with breathless interest, as the two ships raced through the black skies.

Once again the ship was rocked as a blast took effect just to the stern of it. It had not been hit, but so terrific was the concussion it threw the ship around as if it were a leaf. The gunners in their ship were not losing time or motion. Despite the suddenness of the pilot's maneuvering, they triggered their guns as calmly as though the ship was on the ground. A voice, loud, yet with that quality that told it was coming from a speaker announced its presence:

"This is Jetto, your chieftain! I give you one chance to come back. Or I will have you destroyed."

Number 1's eyes closed, as if in prayer. But the words were calm, as if he had long had them under consideration:

"Blast away! We damn you! And whatever you do!"

"Then die, traitors!"

Norton's eyes went wide when he saw what the other ship was doing. As if in answer to his wonder, there came over the speaker, Jetto's command to the pilot of the pursuing ship:

"Ram them!"

It was a command to suicide! And the pilot obeyed, blindly and without question. He turned the nose of his ship in their direction and put the throttle full speed ahead.

They had been miles apart. But in the twinkling of an eye, the distance narrowed as if by magic. The speed was not the only thing that held Norton spellbound. It was the simple physical fact of the ship's approach. It had been the size of a pea, a silver pea in the black of space. Now it was a silver orange—now the size of the moon—then it seemed to fill all of the universe. And the Murian at the controls of their ship seemed to be completely unaware of their danger.

"The button—on that panel in front of you," he said suddenly.

Norton roused from the spell of approaching doom.

"Yes?"

"Press it when I give the word."

Norton didn't have to wait more than a second.

"Now!" came the command.

They were so close, Norton saw the face of the pilot. Saw the look on his face. It was as if terror, fear, hatred and an odd look of resolve were struggling for supremacy, all the while his hands were at the throttle.

Norton's fingers pressed at the button, pressed so hard it seemed as if he was going to drive it through the instrument panel. Then the whole sky was filled with an orange glare. Something in the center of that glare glowed with the bright whiteness of molten metal. Then they passed through the brightness and he heard the sound of things metallic striking against the sides of the ship.

He had blown the other ship to bits with one blast of his gun!

A voice shrieked imprecations at them, "Damn you. You won't get away with this, Number 1. I have your son; don't forget! Come back or by the Four Forces, I'll have him torn to bits."

The pallor of the pilot's face was pitiful to see. But the lines of determination on his face only deepened as he savagely twisted at the knob of a dial. The voice was no longer heard.

"Be there in a short while. Any place you want us to come in to?" the pilot asked.

Norton looked bewildered—as if he were in a fog. The other noticed the look of bewilderment.

"Just name the place," he said. "I'll put us down there."

"It's just outside Los Angeles," Norton said.

Once again the other twisted at a knob and the ship's nose went down. Instantly it was daylight. And Norton saw the familiar serrated edges of the Rockies below. And in the twinkling of an eye, the blue waters of the Pacific were meeting his gaze.

CHAPTER SIX

HE PEERED intently through the glass. There it was, gleaming in all the colors of the rainbow, Los Angeles. Slowly the torpedo-shape descended. And a dozen planes rose to meet it. The Murian's lips tightened, and his brows drew down into a frown. All their plans could go for naught if they opened fire without first permitting them to land. He knew such would have been the case on Pa-Mura. It was the moment they had not taken into account and a moment that tried their souls.

But the planes, which met them, came only as harbingers of welcome. But Norton noticed, as did the Murian, that the pilots had their guns stripped for action…in case.

They followed the torpedo-shape down, until it came to rest on the concrete of the huge airport.

Norton was the first to step from the hatchway. And the first face to greet his eyes was the dour one of one of his dearest friends, Eldon Hale.

Hale's recognition was instant.

"Dale Norton," he gasped. Then as Witson followed Norton, "Jarvis Witson, by all that's holy!"

Then they were a close knit group, pounding each other's shoulders. Norton released himself from his friend's grasp and looked curiously about him. The airport was filled with armed men. Hundreds of the jet-propelled planes he had invented for the government were parked on the several aprons of the runways.

"What goes here?" he asked.

"What goes!" Hale parroted. "Good heavens, man! Where have you been in the last few weeks, that you ask that?"

The concerted shout of thousands of voices made Norton whirl about. He saw the reason for it. The Murians had descended from the ship. Quickly, he ran to the group and throwing his arms about the shoulders of their leader, pulled him with him. The rest followed.

"This is…" he stopped short, realizing that he had not the time for detailed explanations. He was going to introduce the Murian by the number he was known as. "This is my friend. *Our friend!* He is going to help us against our enemies."

"Then you know about what has happened?"

"Perhaps more than you," Norton said. "What's the idea of all these ships out here?"

"Why—we were going to try to get through to the east," Hale replied.

"You mean this is the first time that you have tried to get through?"

"No! But this time we were determined to succeed."

"Wouldn't have done any good. You'd have been so many pigeons for them. Uh, uh. I've got other plans. Give them orders to stand by. Then we'll go over to your place and talk over my plans and we'll see what you think of it."

Several men in uniform had come over while Norton and Hale were talking and had listened in on the conversation. Norton recognized one of them as one of the highest-ranking officers in the army air force.

"So you have something in mind for them, eh, Norton," the officer said.

"That's right, General. I warn you, however, that my plans are neither orthodox, nor in a strict sense, military. But in the present case they will work for the best—at the least cost."

"Then I'll be glad to hear them," the officer replied.

Hale put his home completely at the disposal of Norton and his friends. Witson experienced a complete letdown after the hectic weeks he had spent. But Norton felt exhilarated and rejuvenated at the realization that here at last was the chance for action. He had taken a bath and had changed his garments for clean ones. He was clean, although his skin was still showing the bruises and discolorations of the beatings he had taken. He had found an old beret, which he put on to cover the hideous scars of his lacerated scalp.

THE living room of the Hale home faced the sea, from the hilltop on which he had built it. It was a peaceful scene. The terrors of the past were a long time past in the quiet of the room. But in the tense features of the men grouped around the huge table was to be seen a fear of the future. They knew how terrible was the enemy's power.

The eight Murian mutations were grouped in a body at one end of the table. Norton deliberately joined them. The quiet murmur of voices died down at his entrance.

"Gentlemen," Norton began in somber tones. "I think we can leave what happened to the historians. What we are or should be interested in, is the future. From personal observations, backed up by the intimate knowledge of my friends here, I can say with certainty that we haven't the slightest chance of waging a successful war with the means we have, such as planes, tanks and guns. No. The fastest plane I have ever devised is no match for even one of their freighters. If Jetto, their leader, so choses, he can devastate this entire continent. Luckily, he doesn't want to do that just yet. He is interested in one thing only, at the present time. A region in the heart of the Bad Lands of Utah.

"I say a region because I cannot be more specific. Only my friend here," he placed his hand on Number 1's shoulder, "knows the *exact* location. I imagine that after our escape, Jetto realized that he had best get to this region as quickly as possible. Tell me," he turned to the Murian, "do you think he'll be able to find the city without your help?"

"Yes," the Murian said. "He knows the approximate area. And he has certain men in his party who can determine the exact spot after certain calculations. But that will take a while, *after they reach the general location.*"

"That's the answer I was hoping for," Norton said enthusiastically. "Now here's what I have in mind. This Jetto will see to it that any interference from the air will be suicidal. I imagine he will post air patrols to cover any large scale land attempts to reach him, attempts by tanks for example, or truck. That type of mobile warfare is out. But we have a means that can avail. *The Westerner!* The horseman!"

The men around the table had been giving him undivided attention all the time he had talked. But at the mention of horseman, a hubbub of talk broke out. Some ridiculed the idea. Others spoke for use of air power, still others urged mobile troops against the enemy. Then a voice broke against the general talk:

"It makes sense!" the ranking General said. "And I for one am for it. Let's hear Norton out."

"Thank you, sir," Norton said. He waited for silence to fall, his tall figure, vibrant with a hidden power, arresting in its confidence. They fell under the spell of it as he continued to give the details of his plan. "The three bordering states of Arizona, New Mexico and Nevada were all cavalry stations not so long ago in the past. It is only in the last few years that they have no longer been used as such. But the government still maintained large stocks of horses there. Am I right, General?"

"Right."

"Then I propose that as the commanding officer in this area you commandeer those stocks. Send authorizations by messenger in fast patrol planes. We'll use every cowboy, every old cavalry man, any and all who can ride a horse."

He left his place at the table and walked over to the walled section of the room. A huge map of the western states hung suspended from the ceiling. Norton pointed to three cities on the map and continued:

"At Goldfield, Nevada; at Santa Fe, New Mexico; and at Falstaff, Arizona; we will establish staging bases for the assemblage of our horse cavalcade. Everything will be done at night so as to escape all attention from Jetto's men. Time, however, is the essence of which our success is distilled. Sir," he asked the General, "do you think that you will be able to establish the proper contacts and correlate all activities in a week?"

"Yes," came the succinct answer.

"Good. For that is all it should take for me to do my part. As you gentlemen know, my field is thermodynamics. I had completed a new heat ray, an improvement on the one that I invented for jet-propelled vehicles, and decided that I needed a vacation. Hale, I hope you still have those blue prints?"

"That I have, my friend," the dour-faced man said smiling broadly. "And as your partner, I thought that since the plans were complete we might just as well put the machines into production. After all, their purpose was to provide this country with a weapon that would make it invincible in war. Yes, Dale, I wanted to surprise you on your return."

Norton's face was alive with joy. Good old sour-face! Wait till Jetto got a taste of these things! They'd make his blast guns seem like toys!

"How many have we?" he asked.

"Enough to equip all the men the General can give us."

"There you are, sir," Norton said.

"Leave it to me. One week…"

CHAPTER SEVEN

FIVE days later, a huge cavalcade of motor cars left Los Angeles by three different roads. They left in the still and dark of night. And each section of these motorcades had a different destination. In the lead car of the one bound for Santa Fe, were Norton, his Murian friend, and Witson. The smooth surface of the concrete led for speedy driving. Norton's plans called for their arrival before the night had ended.

"It'll be almost impossible to detect us," Norton explained. "We'll travel without lights. Each car has had a special paint job that will not reflect light and more, so camouflaged that from the air, they will seem part of the ground."

"You did a wonderful job, Dale," Witson said.

"Thanks. But the real job will come when we arrive in the area of operations. If our schedule works as planned, we should be an army of ten thousand men. Enough! What do you think, my friend?"

The Murian, to whom Norton had addressed the question merely shrugged his shoulders. He knew the power Jetto held and was capable of letting loose. And Norton's weapon was untried, as yet. Until he saw it in effect, he couldn't answer. His thoughts were also on his son, captive in the hands of the tyrant. He shuddered inwardly. If anything happened to the boy...

Norton saw the look of concentration and guessed the reason for it. His own face mirrored the grim determination in his breast. *Jetto and his minions must be wiped from the face of the earth.*

It was the hour before dawn when the caravan of cars entered the outskirts of the picturesque city. At the very edge of town a roadblock had been established. Armed men in nondescript clothes patrolled the highway. Some were mounted, some, afoot. Hooded flashlight gleams broke the blackness of night. Their car stopped at a command given by several men. One of them came forward and thrust his head in through the window. In the dim light, Norton saw only a beaked nose and slitted eyes.

"Norton?" the man asked.

"I'm Norton."

"Good. Right on time. Colonel Conners and his men are in the X-2 corral. We've got markers on the road. Follow it until the marker to the cut-off. Somebody there'll direct you to quarters."

The road led through the heart of town. There was an odd holiday air manifest. People stood about in large groups. Mounted men rode in constant parade through the main street. Voices came to them, like the distant murmur of a muted wind in the first blow of a storm.

A highway marker gleamed momentarily and showed that the road took a turn at that point. A half dozen men were stationed there as traffic guides. Their flashlights waved them around the curve. Another few minutes and they were in open country. Then another road block. Once more a face in the open window, this one chubby, with open, grinning, mouth showing snuff-stained teeth.

"Yore Norton, reckon. The boss man's waitin'. I'll ride the sideboard—show ye the way."

The X-2 was the largest ranch in all New Mexico. A wire fence opened in a modest sort of way to the tremendous acreage it encompassed. Norton became aware of a vast movement in the semi-dark area of the huge compound. There was the constant sound of whinnying horses and the smell of their sweat. The road led in a winding path to the center of a large cluster of low-roofed houses.

"This is it," said their guide.

A tall, slender man, lean with the taut hunger look of an athlete, detached himself from the group of uniformed men huddled around a large, plain table, on which Norton caught a glimpse of maps. He advanced with outstretched hand.

"I'm Conners," he said.

Norton grasped the hand and introduced his companions. Conners gave the Murian a masked look of curiosity but only nodded in greeting.

"Well, Colonel," Norton said. "I've combed all of Hollywood for men who could ride and shoot. There are six hundred of us out there."

"And a thousand here," Conners volunteered. "All armed," he continued in afterthought.

"Fine. So are we. Ought to be a good party."

"Right. Well, let me introduce you around. Then we'll show you our schedule of operations.

NORTON saw in the first seconds of the introductions that these men had been handpicked for the job. There was something in their faces and bearing that told him they seemed to have all been cast from the same piece of bronze; they had that look of indestructible hardness about them.

"Shall we get down to business?" Conners suggested.

Norton nodded and they gathered around the table. There were several scale maps of the region. Conners pointed to an area on one of the maps and said:

"This is the focal point of our drive, right?" he asked in appeal to the Murian.

"Right."

"Okay. Colonel West and about twelve hundred regular cavalrymen will start from Flagstaff in six hours, approximately noon. Special Indian guides will take details of thirty men each, over appointed trails until they reach," he pointed to a spot marked in red on the map, "here." Of course we broke up the battalion into groups to avoid crowding the highway, thus making it less suspicious to any prying patrol.

"The first group should reach the rendezvous at sunset and the last at about midnight. That spot is our junction point. General Sanders, being at the closest point of contact, will not leave until noon. As you see, we've got these maps drawn to scale. Each group leader will have one. The final phase will begin, of course, when we make our contact with General Sanders."

"The army thinks of everything," Norton said in admiration.

"Not quite," Conners said in reminder. "We never thought of an invasion from space."

"N—no," Norton drawled. "Nor did any one else."

"Send Chief Tall Pine in," Conners commanded the orderly standing at the door.

Chief Tall Pine was a Navaho. He was dressed in faded whites. A brilliant feather protruded from a brightly colored headband. His smooth, bronze colored features were immobile. He stood, silent, waiting for Conners' words.

"Your men have their instructions, chief?"

"Yes. We are ready to leave at any time."

Norton's brows lifted at the chief's use of English.

"Good," Conners said. "Then let them take the first detail."

The chief turned and without another word, left.

"Of course you and your friends will be in our party," Conners said, as he turned from Norton and stepped to a bench along the wall. He grabbed a hat that was sitting on the bench.

His words had been a signal for departure. The other officers selected the map they needed from the pile on the table. And suddenly the room was full of small talk, the kind common the world over when a tension has been broken. One by one the others left until all that remained was Norton and his friends and Conners.

"Good men, eh?" Norton asked reflectively.

"The best," Conners answered and snapped the switch to the room lights.

"Oh, by the way, Norton," the Colonel said as they stood on the path and waited for their mounts. "We sent out those large caliber guns, by pack animals, earlier this evening."

"Large caliber guns?" Witson asked.

"Yes," Norton explained. "Hale made up thirty of them on my order. You see, I remember that ray Jetto used. Number 1 told me that certain ships only carry that weapon. They have distinct markings. And they must fly at a constant speed and at not too high an altitude. The night that we put you to bed early, we went over to the General's quarters and our friend drew a picture in color of the ship. The men who are going to operate these new guns are picked anti-aircraft specialists. Those Murian ships will be clay pigeons for those boys."

Conversation broke off as their mounts arrived. But Witson had no doubt that Norton had not forgotten a single thing that would cause the enemy trouble. Norton had that type of mind and thoroughness. Their horses betrayed a nervousness, as if they sensed the coming struggle and realized that they were to be part of it. A shadow, which dissolved into two separate beings, an Indian and a horse, slid to a stop before them. It proved to be their guide.

They could hear all about them the varied sounds of men engaged in the acts of getting away, and co-mingled with the low-voiced commands were the sounds of horses being saddled and mounted. In an amazingly small time all was in readiness. A pregnant silence settled over the compound. Then Conners stood erect in his saddle and shouted:

"All right, boys! Let's go!"

A SINGLE concerted shout met the announcement. Then there was a vast clattering sound as hundreds of horses moved into action. Not all left by the gate through which Norton's car had come. In fact only a small part of them left that way. Among them was the group of which Conners was the head.

While Norton rode his horse up alongside the Colonel's, Witson reined in beside the Murian, who was obviously ill at ease.

"First time on a horse?" the old man asked.

The other shook his head, dumbly. He was too engrossed in the business of just staying mounted. No one had thought that he might not have any knowledge of horses. Nor had he.

"Yes," he replied to Witson's question. Then, as the horse leaped forward, following the pace set by the lead animal, he continued in jerks, "We—don't—have—animals...*ohh!*" the exclamation was wrung from him as his mount settled into a long-strided run.

"Just let him have his head," Witson called in advice, spurring his own horse alongside. "There. That's better," he continued as the other took his advice.

Their Indian guide suddenly cut off from the highway. From then on it was sage and sand. They settled down to a steady pace, which ate up the miles. The sun was exactly overhead when the Indian pulled up to a halt in the lea of a narrow gully. They dismounted and the men took their rations from the saddlebags. They ate them cold. To Norton, unused to riding such as he had been through, it seemed but a moment had passed when Conners arose and looking at the watch on his wrist said:

"Time to move, men."

They were an odd lot as they wearily arose and remounted. A half dozen cowboys in the soiled jeans and Levi's, which was their standard dress; two platoons of men in the speckled, khaki coveralls that were their desert uniform; three men, heavy set and placid-looking, who were deputies in peace time; and Norton and his two friends made up the Colonel's party. Only the Indian, the perfect example of the stoic, showed no strain from the ride.

Once again they were in the saddle and on their way. Once again the sand arose in dusty fountains from the horses' hoofs. And once again the land rose and fell in even waves before them. This time, though, each succeeding hill was a little higher than its neighbor. The sun descended in the brilliant flaming glow of flame, which characterized it in that part of the country. The sky was like something taken from a calendar. But Norton and his friends were too weary to take much notice of its beauty.

THE night stole upon them, chill and forbidding.

Once again they rested, this time for an hour. And once again the interminable ride. This time they did not stop until dawn knocked at the peaks of the mountains into which they had come. The Murian slid from his saddle and lay inert on the ground, too spent to move. Norton flopped beside him as did Witson. One of the cowboys built a small fire and two of the cavalrymen made breakfast for the rest. It was a welcome relief from the rations they had had on their last two stops. Conners let them rest a little longer, this time. At last he rose and came over to sit beside Norton and his friends.

"About eighty miles more," he announced in a mild tone, as though describing the crossing of the street.

"To where?" Norton asked.

"To where we meet the others."

"And where precisely is that?"

"Just this side of the Utah border. That's why we started at different times and why some had to take cars to get to the rendezvous. We've gone around two hundred and fifty miles, so far."

"What is it, some small town?"

"Lord, no. Although there will not be the ten thousand men we expected, there will be some odd six thousand. And that many men in a town the size of these border hamlets would be noticed from the air. No, we meet in a valley that our friend here," he thumbed toward the

Murian, "says lies about a hundred miles south of our goal. Moreover, he gave us the exact details of the spot."

Conners pulled several maps from the trouser pockets of his coveralls and spread them out for their perusal.

"See," he said, pointing to a heavily underlined section, "this is the valley. It's about ten miles across and half as broad. At its head is a pass, which is a wasteland. Beyond the pass is a great area of desert land, never before mapped. And here," he pointed to a dozen radiating red lines from the focal point of the wasteland under discussion, "are the routes we take."

"Sounds complicated," was Norton's observation.

Conners sighed. "It is."

He arose and gave the signal to resume their ride. The rest seemed to have worked miracles. For even the Murian seemed more at ease in the saddle. Conners was right. Norton's watch showed twelve, when they reached the head of the valley.

Norton looked curiously down into the shallow floor of the valley. Never had he seen so many men on horseback. The entire floor was alive with mounted men. More and more of the thirty-men details kept riding down to join the others. The Murian had picked an excellent spot. The valley was in effect a huge box. The entire floor was level, so that it made for easy handling of the large numbers of horsemen. Far ahead and seen through a haze, was the entrance to the pass Conners had spoken of.

Then the Indian led the way down.

Everything moved with clockwork precision when they reached the valley floor. Two cavalrymen greeted them and after inquiring as to their number, directed them toward one side.

"You'll find herders at number two campsite, sir," one of them said.

"Where can I find General Sanders, Private?" Conners asked.

"Headquarters is just beyond that stand of trees, sir," the Private answered.

Conners put the group in charge of one of the non-commissioned officers in their group and with Norton and his friends in tow, made for headquarters.

The General's face was alive with good humor and his eyes crinkled in greeting.

"Welcome..." he shouted in jovial tones. "Welcome, welcome. Norton, your friend is a genius—a genius..."

"Excuse me, sir," a voice broke in.

"Yes, Lieutenant?" the General turned to the officer who had broke in.

"Colonel West has just come in," the young-looking officer said.

"Good. Send him in."

While they waited for the Colonel's arrival, Sanders rolled down an immense map, which hung suspended from one of the canvas walls.

"Step this way, gentlemen," the General said.

They crowded close to the wall. Norton saw that the map represented the immediate vicinity of the valley and an area not more than a hundred miles on all sides, as was shown by the scale at the bottom of the map.

The tent flap parted and a short, roly-poly man came through. There was something vivacious about his way of stepping, as if he was in the midst of a dance. His features, too, were alive with an inner joy, in contrast to the rest, even the General, who in spite of his air of joviality, had a suppressed air of tightness about him.

The Colonel had a high pitched voice, in keeping with his appearance.

"Maps again, eh, Sam?" he said in familiar greeting.

"That's right. And you'd better get a good look at this one. I'm sending the first of the scouts out to get the lay of the land. As soon as they come back, the first detail will follow."

"Carry on then," West said.

The General lifted a pointer from the wooden edge at the bottom of the map.

"As you will note, gentlemen," he began, "this is a map of our operational area. According to the information given us, this area marked "A," is the goal we must attain. It's a shallow, circular valley, flat for almost all of its surface, and it's approximately twenty miles across. Precipitous bluffs surround it in its entirety.

"Those numbers marked off in red are troop disposal locations. I hope you have driven home to your junior and non-commissioned officers the fact that they *must* memorize all of these locations. The signal corps will use the heliograph apparatus since we have been told that any mechanical signal devices will be detected. The attack will begin at exactly 1700 hours. Now, are there any questions?"

"Yes," Conners said. "Why must we wait for the scouts? Why not go in and beat the hell out of them now?"

"Because we don't know whether they have arrived or not. We have reports to the effect that some of their planes have been seen. But we must have knowledge of how this Jetto is deploying his forces."

There were no other questions.

"You will find dinner waiting in the mess," the General announced. "I imagine most of you can use a hot meal."

'There were no dissenting voices.

CHAPTER EIGHT

THE moon was a brilliant silver disc. Norton, lying on his stomach in the scrub grass looked down into the valley. Beside him lay the Murian, Number 1. Farther off about ten yards, Witson kept Conners company. The silence was broken only by the small sounds of men seeking more comfortable positions in the tough grass and among the boulders. Norton knew that several hundreds of such groups were scattered all around the rim of the valley.

Down below, the moon reflected on the shapes of a hundred cigar-shaped spaceships. Fires made light the entire valley floor. At the very center of the valley, a half dozen gigantic machines showed distorted, grotesque shadows along the floor. He looked at his watch. Another hour of waiting, then—he steeled his mind against the thought that they might fail.

He rolled slightly and the muzzle of the gun at his side pressed deeply into his side. He pulled it forward and then Murian turned at the sound.

"You feel pretty certain that this weapon will do the trick?" he said.

"Yes..." Norton answered without hesitation. "Further, they'll never know from where we're firing, since there are no gun flashes to give us away."

The moonlight showed a slight, yet wry grin on Norton's lips.

"We have a saying in this world, 'the proof of the pudding is in the eating.' It all came out so perfectly on the drawing board."

"You mean," the Murian asked incredulously, "that you haven't even performed an experiment?"

"No."

"Oh good! Fine...a brain storm and a whole world..."

"Wait, my friend," Norton said hastily. "It isn't as if I whistled in the wind. Mathematically it worked out perfectly. It should do the same in practice."

The Murian sighed aloud. "We'll see," he said.

The darkness lightened and from the east a faint streak of pale-hued rosy light showed above the edge of the far plateau. The light grew brighter, climbed higher until the sun itself peeked down at them.

Norton shaded his eyes and looked keenly toward the light. Somewhere to one side of it General Sanders and a picked body of troops lay in seclusion. He turned his eyes away and looked below once again. Already there were the first signs of activity, which proclaimed a new workday.

The thin, dry mountain air had the property of making things stand out with perfect clarity. He saw several men come from a large, low building. They were either the cooks or kitchen helpers, whose duty it was to start the fires going. Then, from another building a file of soldiers, dressed in the tight-fitting clothes of the Murians, marched forth.

A hand wrenched at his shoulder and a voice called in quick accents:

"Look...the signal!"

Norton hastily turned his glance in the direction of the other's pointing finger. A signalman was using the blinker code on the heliograph. Over and over again, the message came, "Commence firing, as per instructions."

Even as Norton pointed the odd, funnel shaped muzzle in the direction of the space shapes, he found time to tell the Murian a final direction in the use of the gun:

"The range is about a thousand yards. Set the catch at ten, aim and fire. That's all there is to it."

It was strange, and fearsome too, the absence of sound. Norton and the rest pressed the triggers of their guns and nothing seemed to happen. Yet down below, in the shallow, circular valley, terrible things were taking place.

WHERE the space ships had once stood, there was only emptiness now. And where the derrick shapes of the huge machines had been, only emptiness remained. Norton felt a sickness come over him when he saw what happened to those unfortunate enough to be caught in the path of the soundless waves. Whatever part of their body was struck just disappeared. So it was that he saw trunkless legs still running in reflex action; saw headless bodies stagger drunkenly about. Then a half dozen shadows passed slowly across the valley floor, like the distorted shapes of pre-historic birds. It puzzled him. Then the Murian shouted:

"Quick! Before they loose the ray on us!"

It was the feared air patrol.

"Conners!" Norton called hastily to the Colonel. "Get that gun going."

A half dozen men sprang from the tall grass and raced to the large caliber gun hidden between two boulders. In a few, elongated, ugly snout pointed heavenward. Norton peered upward to where the patrol ships had separated. Just as the Murian had said, they flew at a rather low level and slowly. Perfect targets. Yet when the gunners released their silent blasts at them, they continued in flight.

Something was wrong. And that something had to be righted—soon. For already some of the planes had let go their cargoes of madness on those below. Norton saw men on the far side of the rim in the first stages of madness. Soon all would come under the influence of the ray.

"Damn them!" the Murian shouted, leaping to his feet. "They're impregnable to sound. And that's what your weapon is, isn't it?"

Norton nodded, too overcome with horror to speak.

"Call Conners, quick!"

The Colonel dashed over as if the devil was at his heels.

"Tell the General to attack," the Murian said. "And quickly, before it's too late."

"You mean have the men go down there?" Conners asked incredulously.

"Yes! Yes!" the other answered with impatience.

The emergency of the moment was too great to permit detailed explanations. Conners did as he was told. And even as he gave instructions to the signalman attached to their outfit, the Murian began a headlong, reckless race to reach the bottom. Hard at his heels, Norton and Witson followed in close pursuit. They reached the flat and as they pelted onward after the Murian, they heard the pursuing footsteps of the soldiery.

Norton hadn't noticed it, but directly below them was a shed of some sort. It was evident that the Murian was making for it. And there were those inside it who were trying to see that he didn't, for from several apertures in the walls, flashes of light blossomed. And the ground all around the running man suddenly darkened as the flame scorched the earth.

Even worse, as Norton and the other charging Earthmen came into the open they were at the mercy of those hidden within, who wasted no time leveling their volleys at them.

The Murian skidded to a halt, and fell flat on his face. For a second, Norton thought he had been hit. Then he saw the other lift the gun he still carried to his shoulder and press the trigger. And where a second before there had been a shed, there was nothing. The miracle of sound, high beyond the power of the ear to get, had disintegrated it.

Conners panted to a stop beside the prone body of the Murian.

"The General wants to know what to do now?" he asked breathlessly.

The Murian rose slowly. He looked about and saw that the signalman was waiting only a few feet away, his mirror-like heliograph in readiness. He pointed to a pear-shaped building a half mile off, set in the edge of a particularly perpendicular section of the cliff, and said:

"Our weapons will have no effect, either on the building or the destroyer ships. They are impregnable to sound. So there is but one thing to do. Take that building…by direct attack…"

"That would be suicidal," Conners said in horror.

"Better death that way, than…" the Murian pointed to the rim of the cliff. And they got his meaning. The ray had now begun to show the harvest it had sowed. A gigantic battle seemed to be in progress up there. They saw men in savage hand to hand combat. And above them, the ships moved in languid, graceful flight, sowing the seeds of madness.

CONNERS turned without another word and signaled to the waiting signalman. Immediately, the flashes went forth giving the do or die command of the Murian.

Not all of the men had stayed above. Great numbers of them had come below. With and without leaders, they came forward to get into close quarters with the enemy.

It was an even battle until the Murians realized that the Earthmen's guns were more than a match for their own blast pistols. Then at a command from someone in the pear-shaped, metallic affair those in the open retreated to the safety of the soundproof barracks. Once inside, they turned their weapons on their adversaries with terrible effect.

All this time, Norton and the others were making at full speed for the shelter of a large steel dormitory. Someone was waving a white shirt from one of the windows. They piled into the structure, guns at the ready. There wasn't anything to be afraid of. Only an immense room, stretching for a full hundred yards, divided into halves, barren except for bunks on either side: there was no other thing in the room. Nothing but a handful of the most wretched humans they had ever seen. They were gathered in a huddle in the near corner of the room, their eyes looking toward them with the frightened looks of those in too great a misery to do anything else.

"You!" Norton called to one of them, the least wretched of the lot. "Any more of you here?"

The man could only shake his head in dumb misery.

"Never mind them," the Murian said. "Let's get to Jetto. Blast it! I didn't think he'd bring a 'Duro' house with him."

"*Duro* house?" Norton asked.

"Yes. Impervious to anything but molecular dissolution. That's why your weapon has no effect on it. And since we're in the comparative shelter of this place, let's plan our course."

"Right," Conners said. "What do you think we ought to do?"

"First take a look at the situation from the other end of this building."

The Murian started at a trot for the far end, the rest following close at his heels. He peered cautiously through one of the windows. Norton stood at his shoulder and followed his example. The wide stretch of ground before them was alive with men, some in the varied dress of the attackers, others in the outlandish dress of the Murians, and all engaged in a struggle to the death.

When a man was struck by the lightning bolt that was shot from one of the blast pistols, he became at the instant, a charred hulk, crisply stiff and black as pitch. The Murians simply disappeared when they came within range of the sound blast. Not all of the Murians had reached the safety of the Duro house.

"It wasn't meant to house all of us," the Murian explained. "You see, it's only about sixty feet high and about the same in diameter. He's probably got his personal guard and all of his council in the building with him. "Norton!" he suddenly yelled.

"What?" Norton stepped away from the other and looked at him as if he thought the other had gone mad.

"Look! A Duro freighter. If we can reach it, I've got a terrific idea."

Norton looked in the direction of the Murian's pointing finger. An immense space ship stood in solitary grandeur where once there had been some twenty of the other ships.

It was quite the largest plane Norton had ever seen. He imagined it was capable of holding a thousand men.

"Okay, pal," Norton said as he opened the door. "Let's go!"

And once again the mad race began, this time for the freighter, which could well be the solution to their horrible predicament. As though the men in the Duro house realized what their intention was, a terrific barrage was laid down in front of them. Since they had to pass the Duro house before they could reach the freighter, they had to get past the zone of fire. Number 1, who was in the lead, threw up his hand and brought them to a halt.

"No use," he panted. "They've got us."

And then a horde of screaming men cascaded down from the hillside behind the pear-shaped house. At their head was the roly-poly Colonel West. It was as if they had gone mad. They spilled around the house, running at full speed and firing their guns into every sight opening they could see in the Duro house. It was a mad thing they were doing—and utterly hopeless, for those within simply blazed away at them in the security of their impenetrable walls.

THE toll the Murians took on the Earthmen was frightful. But it did what was the only thing that permitted Norton and his friends to continue. It kept those within busy fighting off the new danger. So it was that Norton and the rest reached the Duro freighter with fewer casualties than they feared.

The Murian made straight for the hatchway leading to the pilot's cabin in the nose of the ship. Norton had time only to observe that the inside of the ship was as large as a good-sized battleship, and that it was deserted. Then the

Murian was running full speed down a long runway in the center. About a third of the way down he turned down a corridor and stopped before a door.

"If only the automatic motor is in operation," he muttered as he pressed at a button in the wall next to the elevator door.

It was.

The door opened from the center in two sections. And confronting them was one of the largest elevators Norton had ever seen. Low expressions of amazement fell from the lips of the soldiers who crowded into the ship, following Norton and Number 1.

The Murian pressed at another button, the outside doors swung closed and almost immediately they were at the topmost level. The doors came open and they found themselves in an elaborate cabin, empty of humans.

The Murian wasn't interested in what he saw there. His gaze was riveted on another door. He walked to this one, slowly. And Norton saw his lips press tight against each other as he punched at the button beside the door. When the door opened, Norton was sure that the other muttered some sort of prayer of thankfulness. Because what he said was:

"One chance in a thousand that they didn't think to close this door. Now we really have the chance to win."

But he didn't go through it. Instead, he turned and went over to the wide pilot's seat. Whirling it around, he addressed the rest of the Earthemen, saying:

"Well, men. We come to the time for a most important decision to be made. And it's all up to you."

They looked at him, puzzled by his words.

"You see, it boils down to a question of choice. This ship carries a smaller one, a fighter ship, the fastest thing in the universe. Above us, as you know, are six such planes. You have the choice of sending me aloft in an attempt to destroy these planes. If I succeed, then all is well, for then I can destroy the Duro house and all those who are within it. But if I fail, then Jetto, or whoever has observed us, will communicate the news to those who survive. There are weapons on those destroyer craft that will disintegrate this freighter.

"The alternative is this. Man the weapons on the topside; fight off whoever attacks from above, while some of us man the stern guns and turn them against those in the house. It might be a slow death one way and a fast one the other. But death in any eventuality. If I succeed, then all is saved. I leave it to you."

For a moment there was utter silence while the men looked at each other. Nothing was said. Yet somehow they saw in each other's eyes, the same answer.

It was Conners who gave the answer:

"Take the fighter up. Just show us those guns you were talking about."

Five minutes later, the Murian stepped before the open door. Each of the men there had shaken him solemnly by the hand in farewell. Then Norton stepped forward.

"Y'know, my friend," he said as he clasped the other's hand. "I sort of envy you. You see, I too like to get in there and punch away as long as I'm able. And if the odds are against me, so what. I'd sure like to be up there with you, fella."

CHAPTER NINE

THE other looked keenly into the lined and still bruised features, swept upward to the torn scalp, and peered deep within the smiling eyes of Norton. An answering smile came to his own eyes.

"There's no reason why you can't," he said. "There's a gunner's seat in the cabin, you know."

"You mean…"

"Come on, then. We've an appointment with destiny."

Norton watched with fascinated glance as Number 1's hands worked at the rather simple arrangement on the dashboard. It was far less complicated an affair than any he had ever seen. The markings were foreign to him, but he could almost guess what the symbols were. When the Murian pressed the first, home, a distinct humming sound was heard. The second started the slim torpedo shape along the greased skidway on which it rested. The third was on a lever, which the pilot did not use until they were through the hatchway, which the Murian had opened before they stepped into the ship.

While all this was going on, Number 1 gave Norton his instructions:

"We'll have the element of surprise with us. For even if they spot us, it won't occur to them that we are enemies, unless Jetto warns them. Of course we will also hear that warning."

His words sort of trailed off at the end.

"…Let's hope that they're too busy in the Duro house to notice us."

Norton looked through the glass in front of him and saw that they were in the air. The Murian was making altitude slowly. Norton guessed that by so doing he wouldn't arouse the suspicions of the others.

"Do you remember how you operated the gun aboard the other ship?" the Murian asked.

"Yes."

"Well, there's a similar button down below the level where your right hand is. See it?"

"Yep."

"Now I'm going to be too busy operating this ship to have time to fire the guns in my side," the Murian said. "That button operates two guns simultaneously, one in the nose and the other slanted forward from the portside. Keep your finger lax on the button and your eyes glued to the glass in front of you. When you see the crosswires in the center of the glass glow red, press the button in."

Norton nodded his head in understanding and did as he was told. He had thought the glass panel at the level of his eyes was a mirror. Now he saw that it didn't send back the reflection of his face. Yet he couldn't see through it.

A voice suddenly blared:

"Beware fighter ship coming in! Beware fighter..."

And the Murian went into action. The lever, which had been only part of the way in, was thrust in for its full length. Norton was shoved back hard against his seat, as the ship's nose was pointed skyward. He threw a hurried glance through the glass of the cabin and saw that the black of outer space surrounded them. Then the ship's nose pointed straight to Earth and the Murian's voice came to him in soft warning:

"Watch the glass...we're going in!"

COLONEL CONNERS and Witson watched the small, streamlined ship take off. In each heart was a prayer for the success of their undertaking. They could see through the wide-curving glass of the cabin the whole panorama of the sky above them. The six destroyers still sailed above in lazy circles. Norton's ship took a course, which passed them by a good distance. Suddenly the two watchers went tense and pressed their faces close to the glass.

They had seen the six craft suddenly split up the formation they were in, and saw too that Norton's ship had inexplicably disappeared from view. Witson guessed, correctly, what had happened.

"Those ships. They've been warned."

Then, as though it came from nothingness, Norton's ship plummeted Earthward into their vision again. Its nose was pointed straight down as if it was going to plunge itself into the valley floor. At the last second, and as though by a miracle, it straightened out and flew right in between two ships flying side by side. They saw a burst of flame shoot from the nose and side of Norton's ship and one of the two ships became an incandescent ball. It fell in slow spirals toward the ground. But before it could land, there was terrific report, heard within the walls of the freighter, and the destroyer craft disappeared into a thousand bits of flaming wreckage.

A tight grin of satisfaction spread Norton's lips, as he watched the plane he had shot down disintegrate. Suddenly a horrendous sound shot through the inside the cabin. The sister ship to the one they had shot down had caught them in their sights for the barest instant. They hadn't been hit, but the flame had burst just before their nose and the concussion rocked the staunch little craft from stem to stern.

Number 1 twisted desperately at the wheel with one hand while the other pushed at the speed lever. The ship stood on its end, literally and the larger destroyer swept by. The hairlines glowed red in that second and Norton pressed hard at the button. Once again there was that awesome sound of metal being torn asunder, of flame striking the combustibles that made up the other's armament. He caught a momentary glimpse of the flaming coffin that was the other ship as it slid past them.

"Two," Norton counted softly. "And four to go."

Now the air all around them fairly crackled as the flame bursts from the other four ships struck closer and closer to home. The pilots of those ships had evidently decided that in single plane combat Norton's pilot was far their superior. Then better to sacrifice one or two and get him by ganging up on him. The odds were all in their favor.

A weird and thrilling chase began then, for Number 1 was quick to realize their intentions. He was also quick to realize that in that case he stood little chance of escaping. So he put the throttle all the way in and let them chase him all over the sky.

First they sped high into outer space, then they dipped downward in a weaving serpentine pace toward Earth. And all the while the Murian watched in grim fascination through the glass before him, to see that they did not out-guess him.

"I think they've got us," he said after a few moments. "The engines can only manufacture enough fuel for a limited time. That's why the freighter carried this plane. And the ones chasing us are larger, with greater capacities."

"You mean this is the end?" Norton asked.

"Could very well be."

"Then the hell with them! Let's go in and knock off as many as we can, before we go out!"

"No!" the Murian said softly. "We have a chance. A slim one. If your friends only catch on to what I'm going to do?"

Norton gave the other a puzzled look. "Might as well shove over," Number 1 suggested. "There won't be any need of the guns now."

"You see," the Murian went on when Norton moved close to him. "This is a faster ship than the others. I'm going to level it off about a hundred yards above the ground. And I'm going to fly back and forth above the freighter."

"I get it," Norton said excitedly. "If they've got anyone manning the topside guns in the freighter, the ships coming in behind us will be easy marks."

"*If* they've got anyone manning those guns," the Murian reminded him softly.

CONNERS and Witson watched the enthralling drama taking place above them. They broke into spontaneous cries of delight when they saw the second ship burst into flames. Then their delighted cries changed to ones of horror and warning when they saw the flight of four come down on them from above. It seemed the most miraculous sort of maneuvering, the way the smaller ship evaded the clumsy approaches of the others.

Suddenly the smaller ship did the narrowest inside loop Conners had ever seen, and streaked—almost at treetop level—toward them. In the smallest perceptible time the ship with Norton and the Murian passed overhead. And close behind, the four pursuing ships streaked after them.

Again a loop, this one an outside loop, and the pursued and the pursuers passed overhead. And once again.

"What the hell's that fool trying to do?" Witson grunted.

"Don't *know*," the Colonel said worriedly. "But there must be a reason other than one of escape. I'd say their plane was way beyond the others' speed."

Once again the chase passed above and at such a low altitude, that Witson exclaimed:

"Damnit! What's he trying to do, ram this thing?"

"Hmmm," Conners said in a speculative tone. "They're flying so low that it seems like I could reach out and...holy smoke. Witson...I know why they're doing that..."

"Huh?"

"Don't you remember? The Murian told us about the guns on the upper deck and to use them in a pinch. That's why he's flying so low! And directly over our heads. He wants us to knock the others out of the sky."

The other looked at him blank-eyed. But Conners spurred into action. Whirling from the window, he ran at full speed for the top deck where the rest of the crew had gone. Norton had suggested that they man the guns up there just in case he and the Murian didn't succeed in their attempt to destroy the other ships.

Among the twenty odd men were some who had belonged to a crack anti-aircraft outfit. And the last thing the Murian had done was to explain the mechanics of operating the guns.

"You men!" Conners shouted as he raced down the stretch of metal catwalk toward them. "Man those guns. Quick!"

Their faces betrayed a certain puzzlement they felt at his excitement, but they leaped to the guns in automatic obedience.

The entire roof of the freighter was made of some material, which had the property of glass in that it could be seen through. The long muzzles of the guns protruded through the ports set in the material. They could see the planes in the distance start on another lap of the chase. It would be a matter of seconds, then they would be overhead and past.

"The lead one's ours," Conners warned. "Get the others."

Like automatons the men moved to adjust the sights and set the automatic calculators. The whole thing took a few seconds. Just long enough so that they were through by the time the first ship went by. Then the others followed. And twin flashes of flame leaped from the muzzles of the guns.

And then there was only a single plane following the other.

The Murian spun the ship, about. And Norton saw what had happened. An involuntary cheer came to his lips. But when he returned his glance to Number 1, he saw that the other's face bore a look of intense worry.

"Something wrong?" he asked quickly.

"Fuel's about run dry," the Murian said quietly.

"You mean...this is the pay-off?"

The Murian was silent. In his eyes, however, was that which told Norton that the man had come to some momentous decision.

"You're not afraid to die, are you?" the Murian asked.

Norton looked through the glass and saw that the other plane was coming toward them at blinding speed.

"No," he answered shortly.

"Then make your peace," the Murian suggested. "What I'm going to do…well, it will be suicidal."

Norton nodded gravely.

"Hang on then," the other said. And pressed the speed lever all the way in.

The ship responded instantly. Norton watched in helpless horror, as the Murian whirled their plane through the sky. And realized that they were losing speed. He knew that Number 1 was aware of that fact also. He could only wait and wonder at what his companion had in mind.

Now they were going so slowly that the pursuing ship overshot theirs. The other turned back, went up a few hundred yards, so as to get the proper altitude, then screamed down in a power dive. And the Murian turned the nose of their ship up to meet the enemy!

NORTON'S mouth opened in an involuntary shout. But the sound died before he could utter it. He saw the cold look of utter indifference on the Murian's face as he set his plane into the path of destruction. Then Norton looked up and saw the terror-stricken countenance of the pilot of the oncoming plane. Saw the man make a last, frenzied move to escape his doom. He almost succeeded. At the last second, the other ship skidded from their path. But not quite far enough. They struck and rammed halfway into the belly of the larger ship. And a whirling, flame-drenched mass twisted lazily earthward.

A vast blinding light swept the vision from Norton's eyes. First, thunder had boomed in the cabin, then the light. He became a match caught in a whirlwind. The column of metal to which his chair was attached, broke off at the base. His unconscious body swept forward against the strap and broke it as if it were a piece of string. Somehow, he was sent skidding along the floor and in between two supporting beams. And there his body lodged, while the entwined shapes fell to earth.

The flaming wreckage struck the ground in a final burst of flame. And immediately fell to bits, the torn and burning bits scattering far and wide. And one of those bits of wreckage was the cabin in which Norton and his friend had been entombed.

"Nor-ton. Nor-ton…"

He heard his name called, the voice seeming to come from a long distance. Stiffly, his head turned to the sound. He opened his eyes and was surprised that he could see.

"Nor-ton…Nor…ton…"

Again the voice came, this time in weaker accents.

Norton rolled over onto his belly. Slowly, one knee came up, then the other. He rested in that position for an instant. Then he placed his hands, knuckles down to the ground and brought his legs up to a crouching position, and straightened upright.

He looked about him with pain-clouded vision. A few feet away was the twisted shape of something that had once been a human figure. Now it was like a rag doll, torn by the hands of a willful child. The sound he had heard came from the doll-shape.

"Nor…"

He forced his legs to move, although he could not feel anything. The doll-shape kept fading from view and returning, like a mirage seen through delirium filled eyes. The voice too, was now near, now distant. But something commanded him to move to the horror, which was there.

He stood above the torn and grotesquely twisted shape of the Murian. Or rather he swayed in a kind of drugged stupor. But now his eyes were clear. He wished they weren't. It was not right that man should see another man who was alive and looked like the Murian. For the Murian was alive!

It was incredible.

His completely nude body looked as if a thousand knives had been put to work on him. His right arm hung by a sliver of bone and torn flesh, to his armpit. Something had gouged out his left eye and the socket, bloody and oozing slime, had an air of raffish ribaldry. A whole section of skin had been torn away from the jawbone exposing the gums all the way to where they ended below the ear. Only there was no ear.

And this travesty of life lived!

Norton dropped to one knee beside it. The sounds it was making were barely discernible.

"Norton...Norton!"

"Yes," Norton breathed huskily.

The twisted body on the ground writhed in torturing pain. A high, keening sound came from the torn mouth. Norton's flesh crawled as the sound tore through his very vitals. Then Norton said, "It's me, Norton. I'm here, beside you."

HE COULDN'T understand how that mouth and those hideous lips could conceive and give event to articulate sounds. Yet in an instant, in answer to his words, the Murian's good eye opened and focused in a terrible, concentrated look on Norton's face.

"Dying. Dy—ing," the voice whispered. "Got to—to do—something. My boy—in there." The voice became a shriek. A terrible, pain-filled cry for the right to live a little while longer. "Got to—get him!"

"Easy man," Norton commanded. Gently, his hand came down and pressed the other, who had by some means of sheer will power, risen half way erect, back to the ground.

Number 1 was too weak to struggle. Already the thread of life was raveling at a pace too swift for repair. Norton realized it as well as the other.

Once again the man on the ground displayed that tremendous and awe-inspiring will.

"Norton," he said, and his voice was strangely alive, "promise me—that you'll try to get to the boy. Don't let anything happen to him. Don't...let...*anyth...*"

There was no more—of man or words.

Norton stumbled erect once again. He brushed the hot wetness from his eyes. Across the rubble strewn ground a group of men came running in his direction. In the lead was the slender, but no longer dapper figure of Colonel Conners. And behind him a few feet was Witson.

They were a tight-lipped, vengeful group around the body of the dead Murian.

"My God!" Witson burst out. "We didn't expect to see either of you alive."

"Guess I'm too tough to die," Norton said. "Got caught between two support beams and I guess they absorbed the shock of the fall. He lived for a short while. And now we have, or rather I have, a promise to keep."

He told them the Murian's last words.

"It's our promise, too," Conners said.

There was no need for questions. The group turned and followed the two men in the lead. Their steps were led in the direction of the Duro house, gleaming in the light of the sun. They saw, when they came within a hundred yards of it, that it was completely surrounded by the General's men. The dead and the not dead. It was an almost even division. Jetto and his crew were exacting a fearful payment.

Norton brought them to a halt. A plan had formed in his brain, a plan that had to do with the undoing of Jetto.

"Conners," his voice was terse. "Get to the General and have him order a retreat."

"Are you nuts?" said Conners in horror.

"Do as I say," Norton demanded.

CHAPTER TEN

The heat rose in Conners' face at the preemptory command. His throat worked. Words, angry ones, bubbled on his lips. And Witson spilled oil on the troubled waters.

"Softly, gentlemen. No time for quarrels. I think Norton has something in mind, Conners. Am I right, Dale?" Witson said.

"You are," Norton said tersely. "Get to the General and have him do as I suggested. Then bring him to me and I'll explain."

Conners went in person. Soon the signal mirrors flashed their messages to all parts of the battleground. And weary, battle-grimed men lifted their tired bodies from the earth, and moved to the rear. The flashes from the pear-shaped house continued to follow until the last of them was out of range. The dead looked like petrified, blackened sections of trees.

"Well, Norton," Sanders asked. "What's on your mind?"

"Just this, General. I know how we can beat them. And I think it's going to be the only way. Because it's obvious that Jetto and his pals have thought about every possibility or rather every probability in their defense. Including that of having to fight at night."

"You're not saying anything, so far, Norton. It was my thought that we might be able to starve them into submission."

"If they wait to be starved. But they won't! This Jetto is one smart cookie. He's most certainly thought of the same thing. And going that presumption one better I'd say that he also has a way out. And I think I know what he has in mind.

"That freighter out there! He can get all of his men into it. And what's to prevent us from stopping him. Once he's in there...well...he's gone. And he'll be back. When he comes the second time, he'll make sure that he doesn't fail again."

"Wait a second," Sanders objected. "We can stop them, though. These guns of yours have a longer range than any of his. We can blanket the ground from the house to the freighter with our fire. Hell! Let 'em run the gauntlet. I hope they try it."

"Something, and all I can say is that it's intuition, tells me that our idea isn't going to pan out. So I'm offering an alternative. Give me fifty men. And let me do it my way—in conjunction with yours."

"Tell me what it's all about..."

Norton started to tell General Sanders his plan, but an emotional impulsiveness changed his mind. Instead, he stepped toward the troops and said:

"Men! I want fifty volunteers. Fifty volunteers...and remember, we don't have a chance if we're caught by the Murians."

Nearly every man threw his hand upward. The General started to voice a protest but fell silent, a look of resignation on his face. Norton picked his volunteers at random. Conners and West were among them. Motioning with his head for them to follow, Norton started for the steep-sided valley wall.

"Ugh!" West repressed a shudder of repugnance with an effort. They had come across the first of those who had been caught in the maddening rays. To Witson and Norton the distorted, naked bodies were a familiar, but still horrible sight. But to the rest of the men, who, because they lived on the West Coast, had the good fortune to have been missed, they were the most terrifying things they had ever seen. Many of them had been a little skeptical of the stories they had heard.

"That's why we've got to succeed," Norton said.

A QUARTER-MILE from the edge of the cliff was a small, wooded section of land. It was within the security of the trees it contained that they had tethered their horses. Norton said:

"Before I tell you what's on my mind, does anyone have any idea how long it would take to reach that huge overhang of rock that juts out over the freighter?"

Conners' eyes narrowed in speculation. "We'd have to go up this side of the valley and around the rim. I'd say...about five or six miles," he said slowly.

"An hour, on horseback?" Norton asked.

"About."

"Good," Norton said. "Here's my plan. In about an hour, it'll get dark. Dark enough, at least, to hide our movements, in case any of the Murians in the Duro house should be curious about our disappearance. I noticed that there were any number of cowboys among those who made up some of the party. And, I'm supposing that at least some of them, out of habit, brought their lariats along. There's a sixty or seventy-foot drop from the top of the cliff to the roof of the freighter. And if any of you remember, the door from which we flew the small plane is still open."

For the first time, Conners displayed enthusiasm.

"I get it," he said. "We use the lariats as ladders. Get into the freighter and hide. Then when the Murians reach it…"

"We've got the jump on them," Norton completed what Conners was about to say.

"So what are we waiting for?" West queried.

The sun was setting when they arrived on the narrow strip of ground, which fronted the lip of the overhang. The sky was a blaze of color such as Norton had never seen. It was as if the Universe itself was giving them a display of its awe-inspiring beauty as a benediction and a blessing.

They slipped from their horses and inched their way forward to the edge of the cliff. Below, the whole of the valley was to be seen. A thin, far-spread circle of men lay on the valley floor. Sanders' men, waiting for the sun to set. The Duro house seemed emptied of life. But they knew it was an illusion, which would be dispelled at the slightest movement from those encircling it.

The flashing, scintillating colors faded into the blue-black of night. And fifty men retreated from the edge and went back to their mounts. A dozen lariats were taken from the pommels of as many horses. Two of the lariats were tied together to make a continuous rope, a hundred feet long. Then they made two of these ropes fast to each horn on the saddle, so that in the end, there were three horses having two sets of the rope ladders. And once more they made their way to the edge of the cliff.

The darkness below seemed impenetrable. There was no moon. With a suddenness that took their breaths away, a half dozen lights stabbed forth from the pear-shaped house. At first they were broad beams of white light. Then the beams broadened until they covered the entire valley floor with their glow. It was the strangest thing. They could see the upper half of the Duro house. But from where the lights began, nothing was to be seen, below them.

"Imagine," Norton said in tones of awe, "what it's like looking into that glow. I knew Jetto had something up his sleeve. Why—he's got Sanders stumped! Sanders' men can only fire blindly into the direction of the house."

"Best get started, then, Dale," Witson said.

THREE men were delegated to stand by the horses to see to it that they didn't move during the ticklish business of the descent. One by one, they began the slow climb downward into the darkness at the edge of the huge shape below. Norton, West and Conners led the way, each down the respective rope he had chosen.

It was an odd thing that the blinding glare of the lights ended at the very edge of the freighter. And a lucky thing, also. For when Norton and the rest reached bottom, they could not see into that whiteness. They waited in silent impatience for the last to slide down. Then, when they had all assembled, Norton led them around to where the door in the belly of the freighter still was open. Like ghosts, they stole within the semi-dark confines.

The center door was closed, just as it had been when they left. And the lights were still on in the center corridor.

"A dozen of you men take positions flanking the door," Norton said. "And you, sergeant," to one of the non-commissioned men, "close that switch. When you hear them enter, wait for all of them to come through, then snap it on…and let them have it!"

"What about us, Dale?" Witson asked.

"They've got to come up this main corridor to get to the pilot's cabin," he said in answer. "See those ports set in the wall alongside. One of us will keep watch. When the lights go on, we'll come charging out, shooting as we come. From then on, it'll be every man for himself."

"Suits me," West said almost gaily, as if it was the very thing he had been waiting for.

They moved to their designated spots with a stealth, which in any other circumstances would have been almost funny. For as yet there wasn't anything to have made them act so carefully. Yet that was the nature of these men who were engaged in such a hazardous undertaking. Silence and stealth sometimes walk hand in hand.

The pilot's cabin was in darkness. Witson moved immediately to one of the ports. Norton, the last through the door, had left it open a few inches, enough so there wouldn't be any time lost in getting through when the attack came. The main corridor was now in complete darkness.

They hadn't long to wait.

It came so suddenly in fact that it took them by surprise. One second there was darkness. The next, there was bright lights and explosive sounds.

"Here they come!" Witson shouted.

Norton flung the door wide and with yelling throats, the men leaped through. The sergeant had done his work well. He had waited until the door had closed on the last of the Murians before turning on the lights. The surprise was complete. But only for an instant.

For the first time there was hand to hand battle. When some of the Murians had pulled out there guns, another one shouted:

"No! Too close for them!"

The same thing held for the Earthmen. Several had let go with their weapons and were horrified to see that not only were the Murians in the path of the sound destroyed, but those who were beyond them also.

Norton recognized the situation for its worth. And felt a glow of satisfaction. At long last, he was going to feel that he had the tangible in his grasp.

They were almost evenly matched in manpower. Perhaps there were ten or so more of the Murians. It was as if madness possessed them. Forgotten were the weapons they bore. Each in his own way, by the strength of his arms, tried to tear the breath from the throats of his enemy. And where the arms weren't enough, then teeth and knees were brought to use.

It was man against man. No…it was animal against animal. For the sounds that came from their throats were not those of humans. Guttural, bestial, their voices filled the corridor with inhuman sounds.

The men behind Norton, under the leadership of the two Colonels, fell into an instinctive military pattern. Both West and Conners had seen that confusion was the result of their stratagem in ambushing the Murians. So they let Norton and several of the others charge in headlong attack. But they held the rest of the men back until they saw which way would be the best to attack. Then they came forward in two columns, splitting the ranks of the Murians.

Norton leaped into the fray with a great bellow of delight. Ever loving a fight, he was not the one to ask the odds—or inquire as to the chance for survival.

A lithe Murian warrior, whose face was alight with the flame of anger, was the first to meet the pile-driving fists of the Earthman. Norton's fists pounded a quick tattoo against his chin and jaw, sending the other reeling. Norton leered and followed up. And the Murian brought his hand up in a blow, which had Norton not parried, would have meant death. For the other had pulled a knife from his belt. Norton took the Murian's hand captive for an instant, and twisted viciously. The knife clattered to the floor. Then he whirled him around and clamped a full Nelson on him. There was an instant's strain and the Murian went limp. But first there had been the cracking sound of bone breaking.

He released him in time to meet the challenge of three who came charging to rescue their comrade. There was no time for fancy fist work. It was hit and duck, hit and duck. But there were three. And he had to make his blows count. One went down, quickly. But the others came in for more. And before he could twist away from their arms, they had him, one around his waist and the other from behind.

The one in front had buried his head against Norton's chest as to be out of the way of his fists. Norton tried to twist away from them, but they clung to him like leeches. More, the one behind had somehow managed to grab one of Norton's arms. Slowly, he brought that arm back in an armlock high on Norton's back.

And Norton resorted to a strategy he had once been taught. He went completely lax. And the inexorable pressure was no longer there. The Murian thought that Norton had stopped struggling. It was too late for him to do anything, when Norton brought his leg back and kicked with his booted foot. It struck against the other's shin with a loud report. And the Murian released his grip.

Norton instantly brought his freed arm around to grab the one in front of him. But the Murian suddenly shot his head upward. Norton felt the shock of the blow, and felt a wave of darkness swim before his eyes. He staggered backward from the blow. Instinctively he brought his hands up before his face. Luckily! For they brushed aside the knife from his heart. Instead, it raked a long shallow course across his chest. It also brought him back from the edge of unconsciousness.

EVEN before full vision came back to him, he acted. His right knee came up to meet the threat of the man coming in to follow the advantage he had. It caught the other full in the groin. The Murian collapsed to the ground with a low groan of pain. And Norton drew back his leg and kicked him as hard as he could in the throat. He didn't have to look to see the consequences of the blow. The Murian was as dead as he'd ever be.

A voice, panic-filled shrieked:

"Look!"

And the battle ceased for a second.

Norton too, looked to where the others were fascinatedly staring. A Murian had somehow escaped from the fray and had made his way to the door of the pilot's cabin. He stood there for an instant. And they saw that he had his blast gun leveled at them.

It was Jetto.

"Ha!" he crowed. "Now you are all in my power. Damn you," he shrieked. "None of you will live, do you hear? All of you!"

And he brought his deadly weapon to bear on them.

With his first words, it was as if Norton had divined what was in his mind. And even as Jetto leveled his weapon toward them Norton stooped in a lightning-like gesture and had plucked the knife from the Murian's dead fingers and had hurled it with the same motion.

There was a silver streak, which flashed across the room and ended dramatically in a fleshy plop. Jetto's hands tore in a reflexive, prehensile movement at his throat. Then, as he tore the dagger free, the blood gushed forth in a crimson stream and Jetto sank slowly to his knees. He rested there for a second, while all the rest, friend and foe alike watched in fascination and suddenly he went limp and fell upon his face.

Then Norton leaped before the rest and shouted:

"Wait!"

They turned wondering faces in his direction.

He had a purpose, however for his odd behavior. He had remembered the man, called Fu-ta. Remembered, too, that he had been opposed to what Jetto had in mind.

"Is Fu-ta among you?" he asked.

The figure of the Murian stepped forth from among the rest.

"What is it, Earthman?" he asked.

"There is no further need for this continued bloodshed," Norton said simply.

"No…you are right," the other said in agreement.

"Your leader is dead," Norton continued. "That which you came to do can no longer be done. It is useless to fight on. You need to give up…or die."

"And if we do, what then?" the Murian asked.

"I promise justice," Norton said solemnly.

The Murian turned and swept his gaze over the men of his race who were left. It was a pitiful handful. Slowly he brought his glance back to Norton.

"We are yours—to do with as you wish," he said simply.

"Lay down your arms," Norton commanded.

It was done. Swiftly, all of the remaining Murians were made prisoner. And the center door swung open and an avalanche of men poured through. At their head was Sanders.

"I see," the General said, "that you have the situation under control."

"Except for one thing," Norton said, turning to Fu-ta once again. "Where is the boy?" he asked.

"The boy?" the Murian asked, puzzlement in his voice. Then the light broke. "Prime Number 1's son, you mean?"

Norton nodded.

A gentle smile played around the Murian's lips.

"He is safe," he said. "Jetto was going to kill him when his father betrayed us. But I hid him. In the excitement of the battle, he was forgotten. And when Jetto gave orders to come here, I left him in the Duro house. You will find him there."

* * *

The August night was brilliant with stars, which were so bright they seemed alive. A shower of shooting stars fell across their vision. And the boy paused and asked:

"Look daddy! Shooting stars! Where do they come from?"

Norton looked down at the tousled head and sparkling eyes and felt a sadness take hold of him.

"They come," he began and stopped. He remembered another night. And it seemed to him, another life. "They come, my son," he continued, "from nowhere. And they never return."

THE END